Jayne lifted ... stark blue one locked onto her.

His voice had been calm just now, but the warmth in his eyes was not from good humor, or working with her. As Jayne stared, that warmth transformed. For a moment he looked, unblinking, into her eyes and… let Jayne see that he desired her, found her attractive, would equally like to lean across that tiny circle of table and…let their lips meet?

Jayne sucked in a breath. "It's just that, after thinking further, I wonder…" *If I kissed you, would it feel right? And how can I wonder, when you're ten years younger? And if I ever do choose a man to become deeply involved with he'll be my age or if anything, a year or two older. And I wonder why these thoughts come to me at all because I shouldn't be attracted to you when I know it can't be wise for our working relationship. And yet I am.*

"You wonder if that will be an original enough idea to compete with other things already out there?"

Umm… Jayne searched her mind for the thread of their conversation….

Dear Reader,

When I started the story of Jayne Cutter, a career-focused businesswoman in her midthirties, I knew Alex MacKay, the youngest of my three MacKay brothers, would be the perfect match for her.

Jayne is uncomfortable with the idea of commitment and isn't facing the real reasons for that. When she falls for Alex, a younger man, she worries about getting into a damaging relationship where there are age disparities, as her father has done repeatedly since Jayne's mother left the family many years ago.

Alex MacKay was dumped on the doorstep of a Sydney orphanage as a baby. He has two wonderful adopted brothers and they should be all the family he needs. So why can't Alex get rid of the restlessness that plagues him, the feeling that there is something more out there somewhere?

Alex and Jayne join forces for business reasons. Life throws them into each other's emotional journeys, pulling away layer upon layer of self-protectiveness until their real emotions, needs, hopes and fears must be exposed if they are to have any hope of a future together.

Please join me as I take Jayne and Alex on a journey throughout some of Australia's beautiful country, and on a personal journey that will help them both to recognize and accept all of who they are as individuals, and what they can mean to each other.

Love and hugs from Australia.

Jennie

JENNIE ADAMS
Surprise: Outback Proposal

TORONTO NEW YORK LONDON
AMSTERDAM PARIS SYDNEY HAMBURG
STOCKHOLM ATHENS TOKYO MILAN MADRID
PRAGUE WARSAW BUDAPEST AUCKLAND

Recycling programs
for this product may
not exist in your area.

ISBN-13: 978-0-373-17762-2

SURPRISE: OUTBACK PROPOSAL

First North American Publication 2011

Copyright © 2011 by Jennie Adams

www.Harlequin.com

Printed in U.S.A.

Australian author **Jennie Adams** grew up in a rambling farmhouse surrounded by books, and by people who loved reading them. She decided at a young age to be a writer, but it took many years and a lot of scenic detours before she sat down to pen her first romance novel. Jennie has worked in a number of careers and voluntary positions, including transcription typist and preschool assistant. She is a proud mother of three fabulous adult children and makes her home in a small inland city in New South Wales. In her leisure time Jennie loves long walks, discovering new music, starting knitting projects that she rarely finishes, chatting with friends, trips to the movies, and new dining experiences.

Jennie loves to hear from her readers, and can be contacted via her website at www.jennieadams.net.

For the women who have inspired me. If you know me, if you understand about the boots and about blurt mode, then this one is for you. Also for my editor and senior editor for encouraging my career path. I am blessed.

For my daughter. I will never know another woman who has shown strength in the ways that you have and I love you for all of who you are. For my boys. And for my rent-a-kids.

CHAPTER ONE

'IF UNIQUE is what you want, you've come to the right man.' Alex MacKay's words were accompanied by an almost deliberately cheeky half-smile.

A lot of people might have taken that expression and seen nothing deeper than a cheerful, confident young businessman being just a little flirtatious purely because he knew he could.

Jayne Cutter certainly saw those things, although she had a feeling his smile was part of his personality but not all of it. There were depths in the backs of Alex MacKay's blue eyes that told Jayne this man had lived. That he had his share of secrets and history.

At the same time, those blue eyes looked into Jayne's sherry-brown ones with enough male awareness that Jayne couldn't help but acknowledge, even if only to herself, that she *was* being flirted with by this gorgeous mid-twenties man.

He couldn't *mean* the flirting, though. Could he? Because this was a business meeting and whether he seemed not only attractive but also intriguing, Jayne wasn't exactly in his age bracket to be flirted with!

'Unique is definitely what I want.' Her response emerged—low cosy tone and all—before she could stop herself. Jayne cleared her throat and hoped he would blame that tone on a frog in her oesophagus or something. Yet flirting with a man ten years younger felt rather appealingly forbidden.

Not appealing, Jayne! As for the forbidden part—hasn't your father caused enough stress with his mismatched relationships for you to know better than to exchange this kind of banter with a substantially younger man?

'I'm looking for unique pillow gift ideas for Cutter's Tours,' Jayne clarified.

She had to maintain her professionalism. The trouble was, she *did* find Alex MacKay attractive. She had done from the moment he'd entered her central Sydney apartment for this discussion. Jayne was curious about him, about those depths in the backs of his eyes... 'I'm hoping you can supply those gifts to meet the diverse themes of all the tours.' This was the matter at hand.

Jayne didn't understand *why* Alex attracted her to such a degree. She had a very organised status quo in her life. Work came first, social needs second. Golf with Stuart every third Saturday. Dinner or a show with Drew the first Tuesday. Other dates with various male friends as they fitted into her schedule. Now and again she allowed a friendship to turn into more, but Jayne protected her emotions. She'd had enough of that sort of minefield through her parents, thanks very much.

Lately she'd really only been bothered with the

socialising anyway. Her brow furrowed as she mentally considered the contents of her little black book. What had happened to outings with the others?

Troy Carringbar had said he was looking for more commitment. And there'd been Harry who'd 'met someone'. And George had just stopped calling.

Alex MacKay, Jayne. Concentrate!

Jayne glanced out of her home office windows at the fifteenth floor view of central Sydney.

She wasn't avoiding Alex MacKay's blue gaze. To prove it, she returned her glance to his face. 'With a company the size of Cutter's, if you gained this contract it would be a highly successful move for your business.'

Behind the twinkle in his eyes, a shrewd determination surfaced. For a moment there were shadows too, and his brow furrowed and the planes of his face tightened. 'I'm always prepared to consider projects that'll grow the business. And I could do with something productive and focused to put my energy into right now.'

He seemed to add the latter thought almost unconsciously. And then he shrugged his shoulders as though to shed those thoughts and leaned forward in his chair. 'Tell me more about what you're looking to achieve with this idea.'

Jayne wondered why he felt the need to distract himself with work at the moment, but it wasn't a question she could ask.

'I'm putting together a multi-layered approach to improving Cutter's tourist turnover, uniqueness in the marketplace, and to creating enough interest to make us even more sought after than we are now.' Jayne drew a breath. 'The pillow gifts form an important and innovative part of that overall outline.'

This proposal was very important to Jayne. She'd worked over the last two years on various projects that had laid the foundation for her acceptance into the position of a partner in her father's company. Jayne should have received that partnership months ago. She'd done enough work and proved herself well enough to have earned it, but her father had become obsessed with the new employee, Eric, and had backed away from awarding Jayne the deserved promotion.

Instead, he had fallen for Eric's slick insinuations that if Jayne hadn't had Eric's help she wouldn't have pulled off her last couple of work successes. The opposite had been true. Eric had tried to undermine Jayne's success because he wanted to fast track through the company himself and thought he could do that by making Jayne look bad.

What killed Jayne was that her father had listened to Eric. Instead of honouring his commitment to award the partnership when Jayne successfully achieved her last major project for the company, he had said he wanted to focus on encouraging Eric for the moment.

Because of that, because her father wouldn't listen to her and refused to see Eric's duplicity through the nice little 'boys' club' mentality they had going together— because Jayne had worked hard for her partnership and had earned it and wasn't getting any younger and her father was being unreasonable and refusing to budge from his stance—she had decided this was her father's last chance of recognising her efforts with that promised partnership. She didn't want to leave the company but she wasn't prepared to stagnate and be ignored there, either.

'You won't find sourcing such a volume of quality hand-crafted items easy.' Alex draped one arm over the leather armrest of his chair. The other rested casually across one khaki-clad knee, yet his focus and attention was razor-sharp. 'In fact, I'm pretty sure I have the only company in Sydney that would be able to solely meet your demands.'

'That's quite probably true.' Jayne's research had suggested this. And for that reason she didn't hesitate with her next words. 'I'm very keen to establish a business relationship with you.'

He unfolded from his relaxed position and leaned both hands on the edge of the desk. 'Then let's talk about exactly what it is that you need, and work out how I can give it to you.'

This time his words held absolutely no flirtatious tones. So why did Jayne's pulse flutter at the base of her throat and her breath catch?

Because, despite his utter focus, he is still conscious of you as a woman. It's there. You can see it. Sense it. Feel it in the air between you. It's there in you too, Jayne.

'You're very confident for a man your age,' she replied, not wanting to admit to such feelings towards him. 'You can't have been running your business all that long.'

'Full-time for seven years.' He said it with a return of that engaging smile, with complete pride, and added just as frankly, 'If my brothers had been able to spring me sooner I'd have started even earlier than that. I've been around. When it comes to age, I don't think a date on a piece of paper has much to do with life experience or maturity.'

Jayne's father could behave quite immaturely at times, so perhaps Alex's belief worked in reverse in his own case.

'The reputation of your company certainly speaks for itself.' Jayne had made her enquiries before she'd contacted him and she had the connections in Sydney's business world to get the answers she had needed.

Alex's words had put Jayne in her place a little for what she'd said, though he'd done it kindly. And maybe Alex was mature for his years. It didn't change the fact that he would qualify in some eyes as 'toy boy' material in comparison to Jayne's age.

Not that Jayne wanted to turn him into such a person in her life.

'What made you think of offering individual, unique gifts as part of your coach tours, Jayne?' Curiosity lit Alex's eyes.

'I wanted to lift Cutter's above other tour companies. The gifts will cost more than generic mass-produced items would, that's true. But if they're used in the right way I think they'll more than earn back the cash invested in them.'

Alex's brows lifted. 'You know that most of my work up to this point has been in exports of items to other countries?'

'Yes, I've seen the wide array of items on your website.' Jayne had read up about the available items on the site, checked costs. Asked her questions in the business community. And then she'd got on the phone and arranged this meeting. If her father wanted to banish her from work for a week while her offices were renovated, Jayne would use that time to pull this proposal together.

Thanks to Eric's interference, she'd been working secretly on this at home for over a month now, with a view to bringing it to her father as one large overall project, ready to go.

Jayne had discussed the concept of it with Dad on a number of occasions over the past year and he'd been keen, so she knew he'd accept the plans once he had them in front of him. Jayne just intended to make sure her father gave her the partnership to go with that acceptance.

'Our tour figures are good.' She didn't want Alex to feel that Cutter's wasn't doing well. 'We get a nice turnover but there's room for improvement. I'd like to see every tour bus filled to capacity, rather than most of them running with a few spare seats each time. I want a waiting list, more tours running, for Cutter's to be the most popular tour company out there.'

'And supplying people with not only a satisfying tour but also a gift at the end of it that's unique and memorable will help with both those things.' The shrewd approval in Alex's eyes told her he agreed with her.

'Yes.' Jayne met his gaze and gave a slight shrug of her shoulders. 'I have this week out of our city office. I'd like to complete my work on this project before I go back on Monday.'

He nodded. 'From my research, it looks like Cutter's covers all kinds of tours.'

'We do.' It pleased Jayne that he'd studied up. 'The annual turnover at Cutter's is—'

'Somewhere around—' He named a figure very close to Jayne's latest statistical data.

'It appears you truly have done your research, Alex.' Jayne's hopes rose even more. He wouldn't go to those lengths if he didn't really want this and believe it would work.

The only thing Jayne had to do was make sure he understood any risks to him. 'I can't guarantee a contract for you. That decision is ultimately my father's but he's keen for me to explore this concept.' He just didn't know that Jayne was wrapping up exploring it this week, but sometimes an element of surprise was necessary.

Alex searched her face for a moment before that half-smile reappeared and he said softly, 'For the chance to work with you on this, I'll take the risk.'

Jayne's pulse fluttered again at the base of her neck. 'I'll do my best to make sure it's worth it for you.'

Take that in whatever way you want.

You do not mean that, Jayne Cutter. The man is half your age!

He wasn't, though. He was about ten years younger.

And he might as well have been half her age when that placed him in his mid-twenties. There was a big difference between twenty-five and thirty-five when it was the woman looking down the barrel at the latter age. Not to mention, this was about business, not…pleasure?

Not going there.

Jayne let out a breath, regrouped, started over. 'To pin down your part in this I need us to work out exactly what items you can source which will work best for each tour.'

See? She could be perfectly professional. She simply needed to avoid getting caught up in that inviting smile of Alex's.

He watched her thoughtfully as if allowing her some breathing space. 'Have you got stats and demographics of the tours?'

'I have them right here.' Jayne held out a sheaf of papers.

Lean brown fingers brushed against her long slender ones as he took the papers. 'Thanks.'

Was his voice deeper than before? Did his fingers linger just a little longer than was necessary?

They didn't. Not really. He hadn't set out to do that. It had just been an exchange of paperwork.

'You're…er…' A shiver went through Jayne's nerve-endings regardless and sharpened her awareness of him. She cleared her throat. 'You're welcome.'

Jayne couldn't stop herself. Her gaze searched his face. She caught a corresponding awareness before he dropped his gaze to quickly examine the index list before flipping to various pages in the report.

So he *was* feeling this—the way Jayne was. His flirting hadn't simply been an empty, automatic thing that he might have done for kicks, or with just any woman.

Jayne had never shared this kind of exchange with a younger man and a little thrill did run through her. One that she needed to set aside so she could focus on the task at hand!

'I have clear ideas for a lot of the tours already.' She had researched as best she could. 'I'd like your feedback by Friday, if that's possible, but between now and then I need to work out what's needed for two specific tours before I can approach you about sourcing for those.

'Meanwhile, I can let you know what the tour themes and details are for all the others. Then it'll be up to you to suggest what you can supply that will match up. I'd like to be in a position to present my proposal to my father on Monday.'

'I can work with that time frame. What tours have you got left that you need to work out?' He closed the report pages. When he lifted his gaze, it tracked over her hair, where the waves of brown fell against her shoulders, over the almost severe grey business jacket with the hint of white camisole beneath.

This time his expression was quite sober, as though

perhaps he, too, didn't quite know what to make of the sparks they were creating in each other.

Jayne half wished she'd worn something younger from her wardrobe.

Do not!

Do so!

Stop being childish, Jayne. You're a mature woman.

'There are two tours that run very regularly with Cutter's but I've had trouble working out what I'd use for unique gifts for them.' And her choice of clothing was perfectly fine, thanks very much. Jayne didn't even want to think about maturity levels right now. 'One goes from here into the Hunter Valley wine regions and then on to a private mountain resort area.'

When she named the place, he nodded.

'I know of it. I've heard they're bringing in abseiling of their largest sheer rock face soon.' He drew a deep breath that tightened the white shirt across the width of his shoulders.

'Do you enjoy adrenalin sports like rock climbing?' As opposed to the extra-curricular ideas that Jayne really didn't need to have jumping around inside her mind! She dragged her gaze away from his chest but instead it travelled downwards, over khaki trousers and, when he crossed one ankle across his knee, to a tan boot that looked more suited to those extreme sports than it did to a business meeting.

He grinned as though he'd read her thoughts exactly. 'Yeah. Certain activities offer good stress relief.'

While Jayne worked to come to terms with how much she wanted to respond to his flirty words, and to stifle every response that flew to her lips, his smile faded a little.

He'd mentioned that he'd like a challenge to occupy his mind. Though she might not know much about him, Jayne understood that. She thrived on working hard and feeling at the end of the day that she'd achieved her goals. It was that last part that hadn't been working out since Eric came along.

Alex got to his feet. 'I brought some sample items. Would you like to see them?'

'Yes, thank you.' *Step into my lair, said the cougar to the...fly.*

She'd mixed her metaphors, but the overall idea came across clearly enough.

'It's this way.' Jayne shot to her feet and gave the skirt of her business suit a sharp tug. She hurried out of the office and towards her apartment's front door. As though he wouldn't know the way from when he'd arrived! And as if hurrying would get her ahead of these very silly thoughts. *Cougar, indeed.*

Jayne made sure she had her keys in her hand and let the door close to lock behind them. She was half-way to the stairwell, every brain cell focused on not thinking about leopard print clothing or those awful Internet ads about how to catch a younger man, when she stopped abruptly. 'Sorry. The lift is back that way.' She pointed—not with red-painted nails, but wasn't that a cliché anyway?

Well, her nails were painted a very refined coral-pink and Jayne had never worn leopard print anything in her life.

She did like six-inch heels that might work with that kind of outfit, but she wore very elegant black cocktail dresses with those, and she only had the one pair. 'I am *not* that sort of person,' she started, and realised she'd said the thought out loud. Plus there was nothing wrong with leopard print...

Jayne cleared her throat. 'I take the stairs for exercise, but we can go in the lift if you'd prefer.'

'It was a long drive into the city this morning. I won't mind the exercise.' Alex's gaze dropped over her legs to her feet. 'If you're sure you want to do—what is it?— eighteen floors in those shoes?'

'Fifteen, and I'm sure.' Jayne could manage in the three-inch pumps. She did it every day, going to and from her apartment to work. She stepped down the first flight, and then the next and the next at a brisk pace that helped, a little, to release the tensions that came with thinking too much about her working life. It was the same theory as Alex's active sports one, except tamer. Was it the hint of enjoying a good challenge that drew her to him? His adrenalin seeking? Or the tantalising thought of attracting the interest of a younger man? Jayne shouldn't even want to go there! Just look how badly that kept turning out for her father with his younger wives.

Besides, it was Alex's complexity that drew her in.

The cheeky smile, the more sober side, the flirtatiousness and the depths of him.

Great. Now Jayne had defined her interest to cover every aspect of the man's personality. Maybe she should simply beg for his undying devotion right now.

'So tell me, Alex, how far out is your business premises? Do you live close by as well?' Not begging. Not even thinking about it. Not interested in anything other than getting to know him from a business perspective.

He named an outer Sydney suburb that Jayne had never visited. 'I live in a converted warehouse building with my two brothers and new sister-in-law. My business address is close to home. It's a bit of a distance from the city centre but I don't need to make this trip all that often.'

'If you've brought samples of your products with you, it seems you've planned to make the trip count anyway. Here we are.' Jayne pushed the exit door open and turned to glance over her shoulder at him. She caught his gaze just as it lifted from her feet, over her legs and up. And she'd been doing so well with her momentary clarity and focus, too.

'Er…my four-wheel drive is just here.' Did the back of his neck flush slightly as he spoke?

Somehow, the thought of him feeling embarrassed to be caught checking her out made him seem quite adorable on top of all Jayne's other reactions to him.

What? Like a half-grown puppy, Jayne?

'That's a lot of samples.' Jayne shifted closer. She needed to, in order to see properly, she justified. It had nothing to do with puppies. Or big cats. Spotty ones, just as a random example.

Jayne!

'This might help you to think about matches for some of your tours.' Alex drew the first box forward. 'It won't take long to show you through everything.'

Jayne's interest was piqued immediately when he lifted out the first item, a hand-painted glass bowl.

'Oh, that's lovely but I don't know if glass—' Jayne broke off with a small gasp as he placed the bowl into her hands. 'It's not glass, and yet it doesn't feel like plastic or anything else I know.'

He grinned and took the bowl back, and promptly threw it into the box.

Jayne listened for sounds of breaking that didn't come. 'How unbreakable are these?'

'Very.' He explained the materials. 'I'm guessing that flat plates and small fold-away clocks, in the style of travel clocks, might also be useful to you in these materials.'

'A travel clock would be fabulous, if it could be done for the right price.' Enthusiasm bubbled through her veins.

He showed her through the rest of the goods. Some of the boxes contained hand-painted Aboriginal clap sticks, boomerangs, small wooden food trays and other items.

'The Aboriginal art I've seen over the years has been lovely,' Jayne observed, 'but different to this.'

'Different tribes and regional influences affect the

art.' He handed her a set of clap sticks. 'I've been look-ing into some of it recently.'

Did his family tree have some Aboriginal heritage in it, perhaps? Alex had beautiful tanned skin and a few nuances of facial features that might suggest it.

Alex had a lot about him that appealed.

Jayne forced her thoughts back to work and hoped her accompanying smile would be more relaxed than it felt. 'I have a two-year-old niece who'd love the clap sticks. She's into making noise.'

At the end of viewing all the items, Alex closed the doors of his car and locked it.

'I would like to come to a business agreement with you.' Jayne's mind was made up. 'There's promise in these items, though it will take time for us to match inventory to themes.'

'I'm more than willing to give you as much con-sultation as you need.' Alex's eyes searched her face. Awareness, interest, business consciousness, all of it rolled into one in his expression.

Jayne wasn't sure she wanted to ask herself what he might see in hers in return.

How could his examination feel almost like the touch of fingers against her high cheekbones? Over her slim straight nose? And down over her lips before he blinked, and Jayne released the breath that had caught in her throat.

She forced herself to push aside the questions and to go on. 'The toughest part for me now is those final two tours.'

'You mentioned the Hunter Valley. Where does the other tour go?'

'It's an outback tour. It covers Alice Springs, Uluru and other parts of the Northern Territory.' Jayne broke off as a look of first surprise and then narrow-eyed consideration crossed his face.

'Could you take the tours yourself?' he asked. 'Gain an insider's perspective that way?'

It wasn't a bad idea to resolve that problem for Jayne, but how could it work for Alex as well? 'If I did that, how would I give you the time you need for consultation?'

'Well, do you have a laptop and access to your company via wireless Internet connection?'

'Yes, I have those.'

'And I have some of my own…business research I'd like to conduct in Alice Springs.'

Before Jayne could wonder what he wanted to research there, Alex went on. 'We can tour together, cover everything we'd both like to achieve, work on our theme and inventory matching as we go along. You mentioned you need to complete your overall proposal this week. I'll respect your need for time for that as well. If you can do it on the road?'

'You're offering to take these two tours with me?' Jayne would have the chance to resolve her research issues. Alex would consult with her. She could finish her proposal. He would do whatever it was that interested him in Alice Springs. Maybe he knew some colleagues there and wanted to catch up or something.

They could spend five days on the road together,

getting to know each other, endless hours of time together.

Jayne was reasonably certain that the *ding, ding, ding* sound she heard in her head was a warning bell suggesting it might be dangerous to spend that amount of time with a young man who'd attracted more of her interest and attention than any man of any age that she could ever remember.

Alex gave that cheeky half-smile again. It didn't disguise the determination in his eyes. It didn't even attempt to do so; it just went along with it. 'Yeah, I'm offering.'

'Then…I accept your offer.' There. The words were out. Now all Jayne had to do was remember they were out there for business purposes and nothing else, no matter how Alex MacKay's blue eyes might sparkle and invite her to get to know him, be playful, be serious, whatever she liked and whatever he might like.

Alex rubbed his hands together. 'Great. Let's get ourselves organised so we can get on the road!'

CHAPTER TWO

'I CAN'T believe we pulled this off in just hours,' Jayne said as she settled beside Alex in a seat near the middle of the Cutter's tour bus. She was being careful to be cheerfully businesslike, and to not quite meet Alex's gaze. 'You made the trip home, packed and got back into the city. I sorted the tours out, packed and got here.'

Jayne had also changed into jeans and tied her hair back into a ponytail off her face. The more casual clothing kind of negated her efforts to convince him she had nothing but business on her mind.

Alex let his eyes examine her. Jayne had the most beautiful creamy complexion and soft wavy hair. Her age gave her an air of elegance. He figured she had to be mid-thirties. With her soft sherry-brown eyes shining with excitement as they were now, despite her efforts to mask all her thoughts behind a workmanlike facade, she looked happy, appealing and…totally kissable.

Not a thought you should dwell on, or even have, Alex.

Alex hadn't felt this kind of attraction to an older

woman before. He'd enjoyed flirting with her, watching warmth creep into her cheeks.

It was not a smart idea when he was trying to establish a working relationship with her, but Alex was finding Jayne Cutter somewhat irresistible.

'I had good motivation to get organised and back here.' For him, there were two reasons. He wanted this work. Giving Jayne time this week would show his commitment to that. And if he tried to find his biological connections in Alice Springs in person, perhaps he would get somewhere.

His enquiries through government agencies in the area had proved fruitless. At least he'd know that he'd done something hands-on about it. Whatever the outcome.

It had been weird getting the solicitor's notice enclosing a letter from his late mother five weeks ago. Why leave him a letter to be opened after her death, when it was too late to know her?

She'd written to try to absolve herself, he supposed. But all she'd said was that she hadn't felt ready to be a mother. She'd had no family of her own and his father hadn't wanted to acknowledge him. Alex had figured out many years ago that he hadn't been wanted. He hadn't needed a letter to spell that out.

It had been the solicitor who'd told him that Alex's father came from Aboriginal roots somewhere in the vicinity of Alice Springs. The elderly solicitor remembered Alex's mother saying so all those years ago when she'd lodged the letter with him before she'd moved overseas.

On the one hand, Alex wanted answers to questions that had been in the back of his mind all his life. Who was he? Where had he come from? But would he want to know those answers in the end?

There had been a third reason for working hard to get back here on time. That was Jayne herself. She was a beautiful, intriguing, mature woman. Alex was feeling a little...fascinated by that.

'You did well, Jayne. We'll have an adventure.'

Jayne's lovely sherry-brown gaze flew to his eyes, searched and...responded with a softening before she shut the response down. 'Thank you. I did my best.'

Jayne chewed her lip for a moment before tipping her head close to his to say in an undertone, 'I should tell you, for the purpose of the trip I'm Jayne Aldis.'

'So people don't recognise you as part of the company? Where'd you get the last name?' Alex approved of her strategy. He approved even more of the way Jayne's head rested just centimetres from his shoulder.

Alex had indulged in his share of short-term involvements with women. But they'd been casual. He'd grown up in a male environment and he didn't really know how to trust a woman in terms of letting himself get close emotionally. Being dumped as a baby by his mother hadn't helped with that.

Receiving her letter had brought pressure he could have done without and, instead of solving those long-time questions, had simply added to the 'need to know'

that had burned inside him whether he'd wanted to admit
that through the years or not.

A casual fling with a potential business partner would
not only be a really bad idea for him right now, while
he had these issues on his mind, but it would be insulting to Jayne. If she was even truly interested enough in
him, she would deserve a lot better than an unemotional
involvement.

Alex had to push each of the thoughts out of his
mind. Usually he could nut things out very easily but,
with Jayne, it was different somehow. Perhaps he didn't
want to shut his interest down.

Alex turned the conversation back to the woman
seated beside him. 'Was Aldis your mother's maiden
name?'

'No.' She took a breath. 'My mother left the family
when I was fifteen. I haven't seen her or heard from her
for twenty years. I no longer feel any sense of affinity
for her.'

The words were calm but Alex sensed strong feelings
beneath the surface.

'I'm sorry to hear that, Jayne. It can't have been easy.
I grew up in an orphanage, myself. I'm sorry you went
through—'

'I wish that hadn't happened to you—'

They both stopped, and Alex smiled. He didn't want
Jayne to be unhappy or to feel sorry for him and yet he
felt a sense of connection with her in knowing they'd
both lost a mother, even if in different ways.

'Well, it's nice to meet you, Jayne Aldis. I'm looking

forward to this week of working with you and getting to know you better.'

'I'm looking forward to this week, too.' Anticipation warred with caution in Jayne's tone. Her glance moved around the interior of the bus and a smile broke out on her face as the anticipation won.

All about them people were settling in, tucking small items of hand luggage away beneath the seats in front of them or in the overhead spaces. Most of the tour group were Japanese, with half a dozen university students who, Alex had heard saying, had chosen the tour so they could practice their language skills. One of them had seemed to know quite a bit about Cutter's Tours, in a rather pompous way. Alex hoped he wouldn't have much to do with that guy.

'Good morning, folks, and welcome to this Cutter Australia bus tour.' The guide commenced his welcoming blurb and repeated it in Japanese.

Jayne spoke quietly over the guide's voice. 'I think this is going to be really good, Alex. I'll appreciate a chance to gather the final pieces of information I need for my proposal.' Her eyes sparkled. The end of her ponytail brushed against the back of her neck when she moved her head.

Alex wanted to tangle his fingers in the soft mass, tug her closer and lower his lips—

There he went again.

Now was not good timing for this kind of reaction to Jayne. He was in the middle of trying to find his biological roots and process how he felt about the death of a woman who had never acknowledged him as her son. He'd learned that what he'd assumed was some kind of European influence in his genetics—Italian or Greek, perhaps—was actually some Aboriginal history.

He had a rich history in this country somewhere that went back at least forty thousand years. He needed to come to terms with that, too.

And there was guilt because he had his brothers, adopted by choice, and that should have always been enough regardless, shouldn't it? Maybe this trip would bring the answers he needed. Alex hoped so. 'Is this a guaranteed bilingual guided tour?'

'Yes. We run a number of them. They're popular with overseas visitors.' Jayne lowered her voice so it wouldn't carry, leaned closer so their shoulders brushed and he caught the light floral scent of the perfume she wore. 'I know some people might never make another trip to Australia, but a lot of our Japanese visitors do. I'd like to see more of them coming back to Cutter's for further tours.'

The guide began to discuss the view of Sydney Harbour and the Opera House.

Alex drew a second breath and wanted to know where Jayne had dabbed that perfume. Behind her ears? Down the sides of her neck? Across her shoulders?

Yeah, he was doing a great job of shutting down his awareness of her!

'How much return traffic does Cutter's get currently?'

Good effort, Alex. Now, if you could just stop leaning

*her way as though you'd like to kiss her in front of a
busload of people.*

He had to see the purpose of the journey, to turn
his thoughts and attention to that and away from this
attraction to Jayne.

Why did he feel as attracted to her as he did? All he
had to offer her was his business achievement, his connections and eye for things that would appeal to certain
buyer markets.

Alex had no idea how to offer anything else. How
could he offer more? He didn't trust in a relationship
with a woman. His whole life, he had carried the knowledge of his mother abandoning him. Alex didn't know
how to overcome the lack of trust that went with that.

He wasn't against love, marriage, children, happy
families or whatever. But he didn't see those things
for himself. He didn't see how they could work out for
him.

He reached for the laptop computer he'd tucked beneath the seat in front of him. 'Care to look into possibilities, Jayne?'

'Of course.' She blinked, blushed a little. Then she
pulled herself together and said very primly, 'We can
go over a lot of work material while the journey gets
started. We can run some projections.' The bus made a
turn as Jayne spoke. For a moment their upper bodies
brushed. When Jayne straightened, her cheeks were even
pinker than before.

She drew a deep breath that let him know she was

just as aware of him. And her lovely rich voice wavered a little as she said, 'Let's get to work.'

For the next hour Alex picked Jayne's brain about her company, its attitudes towards tourists, anything she could tell him that might help with their decisions about the supply of unique gifts.

'You really know your stuff.' Alex had impressed Jayne; she didn't mind saying so. He'd flirted with her again, too, but she wasn't about to refer to that. Bad enough that she'd flirted straight back. She couldn't seem to resist that with him! 'I've never been grilled so thoroughly about the company and what we're all about. I knew everything I've just told you, but you've made me stop and think about a few things in a new way, too. Our discussion has given me a few helpful ideas for my overall proposal.'

She hesitated, then smiled. 'Without realising it, you've acted as a bit of an ideas consultant for me in the last hour.'

'Everything we talked about will help me with my decisions about gifts, too. It all ties in together. I'm glad we're doing this, Jayne.' He asked a question about the trip inventory and the conversation moved on.

Jayne had to admit that she was developing a curiosity and interest in this man that she couldn't consider smart. They had to work together.

And he's young and gorgeous and why on earth would he want a woman your age when he could have any woman of any age?

Yet, as the bus ate up the kilometres and people spoke

around them and the tour guide sat in his seat up the front and occasionally gave an update of the progress through the countryside, Jayne found herself studying Alex's face. Noting the smile grooves on either side of his mouth. And experiencing an odd feeling that she might like to trace those grooves with her fingertips…

Jayne realised she'd been looking silently into Alex's eyes for a little too long and hastily lowered her gaze to her laptop. 'I'll use remote access to download the data you've asked for from our accounting section. It might take a while.'

Alex drew a mobile phone from his pocket. 'I'll make some calls to my supplier groups while you do that. We're about an hour off arrival at the first stop?'

They were, and Jayne said so and turned her attention to obtaining and filtering out the information Alex needed.

He sat at her side speaking quietly through several calls. His gaze was focused. Occasionally between calls he made brief notes in a notebook.

Jayne did her work and registered every breath he took, the ocean scent of his aftershave and the way it blended with his skin.

The bus slowed and turned off into a lush green lane flanked with row after row of grape vines. The whole area was hilly, green, lovely and picturesque with blue sky overhead dotted with the occasional white fluffy cloud.

A sign over the right gatepost announced 'Winery and Petting Zoo' and welcomed visitors.

'Oh, this is beautiful country,' Jayne exclaimed. 'I wish I'd been taking more notice during the trip!'

'Yes. Very beautiful.' But Alex wasn't looking at the view; he was looking…at Jayne. And then he turned away and she thought he was trying to ignore this awareness, and of course he would want to ignore it. He probably only dated women in their early twenties.

Jayne drew a breath that had to be relief. After all, she didn't want him to desire her because that would only complicate her life, too.

She had Drew and others to take care of her dating needs, and she had her career.

And you don't trust in relationships because you don't understand your father in his personal life, and because Mum left everyone.

Jayne loved her niece Cora, but she didn't expect to ever marry or have a child of her own. Face it, if it hadn't happened by now, it wasn't likely to anyway, was it?

'I can't wait to check out this stop.' That was a much more appealing prospect than her thoughts!

Two minutes later they got off the bus and stepped out into a panoramic scene that had the tour group releasing soft gasps of anticipation and pleasure. Comments quickly flowed through the group as camera shutters clicked:

'It's so beautiful.'

'Look at the animals.'

'I hope to hold a koala. Pet a kangaroo. See an Australian snake!'

'And buy a local wine, made from grapes grown right here, to celebrate this occasion.'

'So are you up for a little wine-tasting and some animal-petting, Jayne?' Alex glanced towards the open area of the petting zoo, rubbed his hands together and smiled his beautiful half-smile.

Something inside Jayne gave way in that moment. Let him in that little bit more, even when she'd tried to keep up her guard. She stepped forward and her smile was probably softer than melted butter, whether she should let it be or not. 'I'm ready.'

CHAPTER THREE

'WE FEEL very privileged to pet the animals. The wool of the sheep is so soft and curly.' The words were spoken in careful English by a woman in her thirties. She was the wife of a Japanese businessman and had introduced herself to Jayne as Mrs Li. 'It is nice to see farm animals and wild animals side by side in the same petting zoo. This is a special experience.'

The woman's husband stood at her side. Mr Li smiled and nodded. 'All Australian animals are interesting. We have emigrated to Australia, but we are still learning about things. This trip is to help us learn.'

'I hope the trip can be fun for you as well.' Jayne continued to chat with the couple as they all made their way to the final stop in the petting area.

From the corner of her eye Jayne spotted Alex. He was a little further back, still in conversation with several others from the tour. They would have to compare notes later. What Jayne had found so far was that these tourists had come for a slice of rural and remote Australian life, and had been doubly delighted to have an opportunity to pet some native animals.

Separating from Alex, working the crowd of tourists away from each other, had given Jayne a chance to try to put her attitude to Alex more into perspective. It made no sense that she should be so overly conscious of him.

'Oh, a wombat.'

'These are less common than kangaroos, I think.'

The couple moved closer to speak with the petting area attendant.

'I haven't seen a wombat up close before.' Alex joined Jayne and gestured towards the petting area. 'Did you want to go in?'

The words were suspended in the moment. Alex's gaze…was fixed on Jayne. A consciousness passed between them that made Jayne want to lean closer, to somehow absorb even more of his presence.

Instead, she drew a deep breath and tried very hard to think wombat thoughts. 'I'd like that. I've only seen pictures of them.' Jayne stepped forward, away from being so close to Alex, away from the temptation to reach out and touch him. 'This can be an experience for both of us.'

'It's certainly being that.' Alex's low words were perhaps not meant for her ears.

Jayne heard them anyway and suppressed a responding agreement. She was having enough trouble trying to keep her distance from him as it was.

Leopard print, anyone?

There were no large or exotic cats here, only

Australian animals and farm animals. And Jayne was getting off the track again anyway.

'Come in, folks.' The attendant gestured.

Jayne and Alex went into the enclosure. Once inside, they were met by one thickset, heavy-duty wombat with small dark eyes, fur similar to that of a bear and a slightly disgruntled attitude that altered somewhat when the keeper suggested they scratch the back of the wombat's neck and behind his ears.

'Oh, he's really quite cute, isn't he?' Jayne bent down to scratch behind the creature's ears again.

Alex grinned and glanced at Jayne. 'Cute isn't the word I'd have used to describe him, but he is interesting, in a grumpy sort of way.'

The wombat made grunting sounds and walked about the area, snuffling and considering the various scents before submitting to one last round of adulation from its visitors.

'All right. I guess I'll pay that. He is a bit cross, but I still enjoyed seeing him.' Jayne smiled as they left the petting area and started towards the 'cellar door' of the winery. 'Most of the tour group seem to be really enjoying the petting zoo.' She glanced about her, forcing herself to focus on the job in hand. 'I did consider animal themes for this tour because of the zoo. But they might not be as memorable for Australian members of these tours and, though the tour is bilingual, it does usually attract students studying the Japanese language. I want everyone on each tour to be completely satisfied with their gift.'

See? She could pay attention to her work. In fact, Jayne usually had no difficulty at all in doing that. Meeting Alex had somehow thrown her a little off course in that respect.

'I overheard you talking with some of the guests earlier. Maybe a perfect gift idea will surface once you get to know more of the people on the tour.' He took her arm as they crossed over a rough patch of ground. Admiration filled his tone as he went on. 'I was impressed with your Japanese. You not only have a beautiful voice, but you can speak two languages fluently. I have some foreign language skills but they don't go as far as yours.'

There was no cheeky smile this time, no flirtatious tone, just a straightforward compliment and statement that he thought her voice sounded lovely. Jayne fell more deeply into her consciousness of him in that moment because of his open compliment.

And, because he was touching her, tingles ran the length of Jayne's arm. She didn't react like that when Drew took her arm.

'Thank you. I studied Japanese in high school.' Jayne sounded quite normal really. At least she assured herself that she did as they stepped out of the warm sunshine and into a cool, welcoming indoor area where several of the other bus guests were already being greeted and welcomed by vineyard staff.

But she'd melted into his side a little as they'd walked along. That hadn't been particularly professional. That had been about her reaction to his touch. 'I figured being able to speak Japanese could only help with my work for the company.'

The words reminded Jayne of her high school years. In the middle of those years, Mum had left. Why did Mum have to leave all of them? If she didn't want to be with Dad, why couldn't she have stuck around for Jayne and her sister? Kept them with her? Or shared them between her and Dad?

Enough, Jayne. It's old news and irrelevant now to anything that matters. You'll never know why she made that decision. What you do know is that she left and didn't look back.

Jayne frowned. Alex had stepped aside to speak briefly with another of the tour group. He turned back now, caught Jayne's attention, and they took their turns tasting several wines.

At the end of the tasting, Jayne made a selection. 'I'd like to buy a bottle of that Chardonnay, please.'

When the bottle was presented to her, Jayne examined the label. She lifted her eyes to the saleswoman's face. 'You're the owner's wife? Do you ever label your wines with logos of animals from the petting zoo?'

'I am, dear, and no, we don't use those kinds of labels. Our wines are well known with the current labelling, so we've tended to stick to it.'

'Could I have a business card?' Jayne introduced herself. 'I'm Jayne Cutter. I'm a member of the family who own and run Cutter's Tours. I can't say for sure, but I might be interested in placing an order for some specially labelled wines at some point.'

While the woman leant down to get a business card, Jayne glanced at Alex and got caught in the depths of his considering gaze.

'It's a possibility,' he murmured.

Were there other possibilities? For Jayne and for Alex?

You don't even want to consider that, Jayne. You need to know this man for work and nothing else. He's too young for you, and you don't get involved with men anyway. Not like that. Not beyond socially and, trust me, the way you've reacted to Alex MacKay today is not some mild social consciousness of him.

Half an hour later, the bus was on the move again, with the driver confidently handling the road conditions. The tour guide, on the other hand, looked a little seedy and Jayne studied him with an inward frown. Had the man been taste-testing the wines on the job? If he'd dared to become inebriated while he was working—

'John, our guide, doesn't look well.' Alex murmured the words close to Jayne's ear.

'I was just thinking that. Did you see him drink? I didn't see him in the wine-tasting area.' Jayne turned her head to look at Alex. Wisps of her hair brushed over his cheek as she moved her head.

His hand lifted and his fingers softly brushed the strands aside. 'I don't think he went into that area at all.'

But Jayne went straight 'there'. Straight to Alex touching her hair, and to wanting to melt in to his touch.

Alex started to lean closer and Jayne held her breath.

'Excuse me.' Mr Li caught their attention from where he and his wife sat across the aisle. 'My wife and I enjoyed our earlier conversation with you. When we stop for dinner we would be happy if you would both eat with us.'

'That's very nice of you.' Jayne turned to Alex. She couldn't believe she'd been halfway to trying to kiss him, right there on the bus in front of everybody. Straight after telling herself, yet again, to get control of her responses to Alex. 'Would you like—?'

'Sure.' Alex caught Mr Li's gaze. 'We'd love to join you for dinner. Thanks.'

Did his acceptance sound just a little forced? Had he perhaps wanted an evening with Jayne to get to know each other better, just the two of them?

Well, the words were spoken and it was probably very much for the better that they didn't dine alone. And now Jayne could settle down and stop thinking about anything other than business.

And layers of a very interesting man.

Not that interesting, Jayne.

But he was. Jayne wanted to know more about his interests, the adrenalin-seeking side of his nature that meant he liked activities such as rock-climbing. Physical activities that would showcase his strength, every manly muscle, a leap-into-life attitude that was very attractive.

Um…where was she again?

And perhaps Alex had accepted the dinner invitation because he was more than over the awareness he had initially felt towards Jayne. Maybe, on closer inspection, he hadn't been that excited by what he'd initially seen in her.

Well, that was good. Yes, of course it was.

After two more minor stops they reached their dinner destination. There were several restaurants to choose from in the small township that boasted an annual koala counting expedition among its highlights. The guide suggested they all eat straight away as some of the restaurants closed early. By the time they returned to their hotel their bags would be inside their rooms waiting for them.

'I would have liked the chance to change clothes, freshen up a little before we went to dinner.' Jayne spoke the words in a soft undertone to Alex. 'That's something I'll suggest could be improved about this tour.'

They were walking up the main street of the township behind the other couple. Even thinking that gave Jayne a strange feeling, for she and Alex were not 'another couple'. They were two business people working together towards a common goal. And separately towards their own goals.

Jayne had banished all those other thoughts. She might have had to work hard to do it, might have had to remind herself a number of times, but she'd got there now. Right. So why, then, was she now almost holding her breath, asking herself whether Alex would take her arm or press his hand to the small of her back as they walked side by side? Why was she craving exactly that?

'Would you be happy to eat here?' Mr Li posed the question as they neared a restaurant that seemed to be quite popular with a number of local residents.

'Yes. It looks good.' Jayne hoped it would be. Moreover, she hoped her thoughts would stop dwelling so much on Alex MacKay. She had to stop this!

The restaurant had lovely little octagonal tables and friendly, efficient staff who coped well with the influx of tourists looking for meals.

Jayne slipped into a chair and Alex sat beside her. Though Jayne continued to chat to their host's wife as she took her seat, all of her focus was on Alex. So much for controlling that out of existence.

'The special menu for today is rainbow trout with herb couscous and butter-sautéed vegetables.' A friendly waitress stood beside their table to offer the menu choices.

Jayne and Mrs Li ordered the trout. Alex and Mr Li ordered a more traditional steak with mashed potato and gravy. They chatted generally about the tour while they waited for their meals to arrive.

'Jayne, I believe you are a member of the family that runs Cutter's Tours?' Mr Li posed the question about an hour later.

Jayne gave a start. She'd been sitting there listening to Alex and Mr Li as they discussed the stock exchange. In truth, she'd been more attuned to the tone of Alex's voice than the words of the discussion. She was deeply attracted to Alex. Now, at the end of the day, with weariness catching up with her, Jayne couldn't hold the admission back.

'I'm not quite sure how you knew—?'

'I heard you introduce yourself to the winery manager's wife.' It was Mrs Li who said this quietly. 'We don't mean to intrude. We are guessing that you're on the tour to study how things are running.'

Her husband carried the conversation further. 'As business people ourselves and being interested in tourism, we would enjoy a general discussion of your thoughts about the tourist industry in this country.'

Jayne felt a little at a loss. She had wanted research, but would these people feel the need to reveal her identity to others on the tour? Or want to know things she wasn't prepared to discuss?

Before Jayne could say anything further, Alex gave the couple a charming smile. 'There's no harm in a confidential general discussion.'

In a few short words he ensured the conversation would remain within acceptable boundaries, and did so with finesse.

'That is what we thought, too.' Mr Li nodded.

What followed was unusual, but useful. The Lis asked questions about Australian tourism. Jayne and Alex asked questions about Japan's impressions of Australia as a tourist destination.

By the time they ate pavlova and cheesecake desserts and reached the coffee stage of the meal, some helpful insights had been exchanged.

And if the evening had been simply that, Jayne would have had little to worry about, aside from the edge of nervous anticipation that would remain with her until she'd put her proposal to her father.

Instead, she had another layer of concern.

Right through the evening, Jayne had buzzed with awareness of Alex and, as their time with the Lis moved towards its end, that awareness only deepened.

Alex is too young for you, even if he is truly interested, and you can't be entirely sure that he is. He might flirt a little with all women who cross his path.

That thought was a lie, though. Because Jayne did know that Alex found her attractive. She'd known it from when they'd first met. And maybe he did flirt easily, but her instincts told her the way Alex reacted to her wasn't common for him.

That didn't mean, however, that the man would want to act on any attraction he felt towards her. And what did Jayne want—some kind of holiday fling? That was not her style.

Jayne was content with her organised male company. She had control of that. She made the decisions, chose her level of involvement.

She kept herself safe of all emotional risk.

And there was nothing wrong with that!

They finished their meal and the Lis excused themselves to explore the township a little more. Alex and Jayne opted to return directly to their hotel.

As she and Alex made their way there, Jayne turned her head and spoke. 'I doubt there'll be a public lounge

at the hotel. But I would like to cover today's findings
with you before we turn in for the night.'

That wasn't an effort to retain his company for longer.
It was the need to gather all the information she could
before spending time working on her laptop tonight. It
was! 'Now that I've got some feedback from some of
the tour group, I've got a few thoughts about the pillow
gifts. It'd be good to discuss them now, if you're up to
that.'

'A brainstorming session's a good idea.' Alex's hand
found its way to the small of her back. 'I'm game if you
are.'

Oh, Jayne was game. She just had to take care not to
pursue some of where that 'game' might want to take
her.

They stepped through the hotel's doors and into the
reception foyer. 'Let's get our room keys and go talk.'

It was just the touch of his hand at her back. They
were only words. Delivered in a controlled tone because he was being very careful not to be flirtatious
with her?

Was it for the same reason that Jayne was being so
careful? Because he really wanted to pursue their interest in each other?

Jayne shouldn't want to forget everything else and be
aware only of him. She'd craved his touch, some physical
connection with him. She hadn't expected to be far too
affected by it when it happened.

'Maybe one of the rooms will have a balcony.' So she

wouldn't have to worry about the intimacy of speaking with Alex inside.

They got their keys and made their way to rooms that were side by side at one end of the hotel. There were no balconies and Jayne opted for his room.

Alex flicked the light switch and gestured to a small table and two chairs tucked into the corner of the room. 'Make yourself comfortable, Jayne. Would you like tea or coffee or something from the bar fridge?'

Step into my hotel room, said the toy boy to the older woman.

Stop that, Jayne!

Jayne shook her head in response to his question, when her thoughts were about quite different things. 'I don't need anything, thanks.'

She took her seat at the table while Alex opened his roomy duffel bag and drew out a notebook and pen.

Jayne *did not* wonder what else he had in the bag, nor in any other way feel conscious of the confines of their surroundings and how intimate those surroundings were.

Yeah, not much, Jayne.

Alex sat down and leaned his arms on the small table, which instantly shrank it to minuscule proportions in Jayne's mind. She could lean across that table and stroke her fingers over the beard shadow on his face, touch his lips and discover if they were soft, or firm, or a perfect combination of both…

Jayne lifted her gaze and found Alex's stark blue one locked onto hers.

His look was not only about good humour or working with her. For a moment he stared, unblinking, into her eyes and their warmth transformed to let Jayne see that he desired her, found her attractive, would equally like to lean across that tiny circle of table and…let their lips meet? This wasn't teasing or flirtatiousness. This was frank, genuine interest.

'I know I thought about having the winery and zoo supply us with wines that are specially labelled for some of our gifts.'

Jayne blurted the words out as though they could somehow save her from herself, from the interest in him that seemed to intensify with each passing moment. From wanting to encourage his interest and return it in response. She sucked in a breath. 'It's just that, after thinking further, I wonder…'

If I kissed you, would it feel right? And how can I wonder, when you're ten years younger and if I ever do choose a man to become deeply involved with he'll be my age or, if anything, a year or two older? A Drew or a George… And I wonder why these thoughts come to me at all because I shouldn't be attracted to you when I know it can't be wise for our working relationship. And yet I am.

'You wonder if that will be an original enough idea to compete with other things already out there?' he asked, but his eyes traced over her face, lingering on her lips.

Jayne searched her mind for the thread of their conversation.

'Yes.' She drew a breath. 'That's exactly what I

was thinking. Originality. Also, not everyone drinks wine.'

'So we keep thinking and keep looking for ideas for this tour.' He rubbed his hand over his jaw. 'We have tomorrow as well before we swap to the next tour, don't we?'

They did, and Jayne said so. She loved that he said 'we' and included himself in her plans that way, and that was perhaps even more dangerous for her.

'What about a theme to incorporate Aboriginal art? You already have some of that in your inventory.' Jayne thought for a moment. 'The name of the nearest town. It's definitely Aboriginal. Maybe the meaning—'

He was already on his feet. He brought his laptop to the table. 'You'd need to confirm any township definition with local tribal elders or a land council, but we can start with a computer search.' He used his USB Internet service and they turned up definitions for the nearest two towns. 'If that second one is correct—'

'Then we could go with a hunting theme.'

Alex closed the computer and set it on the floor beside him. He leaned his elbows on the table and smiled. 'Boomerangs, items in the shape of a spear or spearhead. There are plenty of other things that would work as well.'

He shifted slightly in his chair and their legs briefly brushed.

How did such awareness build and build the way it had for Jayne throughout this day and evening? She'd tried so hard to convince herself it wasn't there within her, but it was.

And…it was there within Alex as well.

Jayne got through the rest of their discussion as quickly as she could, and then stood up and walked to the door. 'I'll say goodnight. Let you get some rest. I still have work to do before I sleep.'

I'll leave now before I give in to wanting to stay here just for the sake of your company.

Alex accompanied her to the door of the room. He glanced down into her eyes. Jayne glanced up. Her gaze fixed on his lips and her heart stood still. She wanted to kiss him, wanted him to kiss her. Wanted it so much.

'Goodnight.' She forced her hand to lift and clasp the door handle.

'Goodnight, Jayne.' Alex dropped his arm and stepped away from her. His gaze was also fixed on her mouth, but his arms were straight at his sides, as though to force himself not to take hold of her, not to touch her.

Not to…

'See you—' Jayne cleared her throat. 'See you in the morning.' She stepped through the door and walked the couple of steps to the door of her own room. With fumbling hands, she unlocked it and went inside without looking back.

Only when she had her door safely closed behind her and the room all to herself did Jayne face her thoughts. She'd almost kissed him. She'd wanted—no, needed—that kiss so much.

That knowledge, that need that had pushed past her protective mechanisms, past her determination to make her own sensible choices and not be driven by the kinds of overpowering emotions or feelings that could take her life right out of control, scared Jayne.

She couldn't allow this kind of lapse to happen. At least she hadn't pounced on him and taken what she wanted like the stereotypical 'cougar' she'd been trying so hard not to think about today. And she didn't miss the potential of Alex's kiss. She totally and utterly did not!

CHAPTER FOUR

'Yes, well, thanks for phoning and...I'll give you a call when I'm back in Sydney.' Jayne used a bright, polite tone that sounded as though she'd utilised it a lot of times in the past. 'We'll sort something out when there's time.'

It was a short conversation, it ended there and Jayne turned immediately to Alex once it was over and gestured to her laptop where it rested on her knees. 'Sorry about that. You don't mind if I attend to this while there's reception for the Internet connection and the road isn't hairpin turns?'

She'd been like this since they'd met this morning for breakfast. Cheerful, businesslike, somehow coming across as buttoned up to the neck even though she was wearing another pair of jeans, a scooped-neck T-shirt and running shoes.

Jayne was making such a determined effort not to be conscious or aware of him that Alex couldn't do anything other than be conscious and aware of Jayne.

Not that he needed any behaviour of hers to encourage him to cross the line. All he apparently needed was to sit close to her. Across a small table in a rented motel room as they wrapped up a day of research and travel, for example. He wished he'd kissed her last night. He'd wanted to even though the other side of him had pointed out all the reasons it wouldn't have been smart to let that happen.

Maybe, if it had, he could have moved past this consuming curiosity.

And maybe it would just have made you want to know more.

'I don't mind. I made a few calls myself this morning before I left my room, but I have a couple more that I'll make now that it's business hours and I know I won't be waking people.'

He'd phoned his brother, Linc, to let him know where he was. He'd told Linc he was travelling with Jayne to get a first-hand look at some of her family's tours so they could make the best informed decisions about the inventory Jayne would need him to supply.

Alex needed to tell Linc and Brent about the letter from his late mother through that solicitor. That the solicitor had revealed that both his parents had come from the Alice Springs area somewhere, his father with indigenous roots, and that he was trying to discover more about his history. He hadn't been able to bring himself to discuss it with his brothers.

That trend had continued today. Alex had kept the conversation light and superficial. He felt guilty for holding back, and guilty about his investigations and the motivating needs behind them. He recognised a cheerful, superficial tone when he heard it, though, and Jayne had just used one on the person who'd phoned her.

It had been a man trying to arrange a date.

Alex hadn't been thrilled to note that fact, but Jayne hadn't appeared to be all that interested in the call.

'That's fine,' Jayne chirped, before her fingers became busy on the keys of her laptop's keypad. 'I wish these last two tours weren't so tricky to nail down in terms of usable themes we can focus on, but taking them will be the best hope I have of digging out something that will work.'

'You'll figure it out, Jayne.' Her business skills were well developed, a fact Alex had noted more and more as they delved into what she wanted from him for her company and the logistics of how to make it all work. Alex drew a breath, thought about not asking his next question and asked it regardless. 'I hope everything's okay back in Sydney?'

Jayne's fingers tangled on the laptop's keys and she stopped to delete a line of text before she turned to him. They both knew he was asking more than just that question.

Alex didn't know how Jayne would choose to answer.

She tipped up her chin and gave him a challenging look that somehow still managed to bring across interest and curiosity towards him, whether she thought she had that masked or not. 'Everything's fine. I date casually. That was just one of the guys I see now and then.'

Not attached, then. Not really.

Right. 'I'm in a similar place in my personal life.'

Jayne knew this now. He'd told her straight out. Somehow that seemed important, whether it should or not.

'Right. Okay, then. I'd better get some work done.' She was a little breathless as she said it.

'Yeah. No slacking on our trip.' The teasing tone went a little awry, perhaps because he couldn't get the deepness out of his voice.

They did get on with it then, though. In the next half hour Alex called four of his suppliers while Jayne worked on her laptop, collating yesterday's information and survey results into files and emailing different bits and pieces of information to his laptop so he could look at it all later while she worked on her overall proposal.

If Alex thought he could ignore her and not think about her, he'd need to sit at the other end of the bus. Because Jayne looked beautiful working. She seemed to look beautiful no matter what she was doing. Her hair was up in a ponytail again. Alex wanted to take it down and sift his fingers through it.

And he wanted to taste her lips and know…

The phone picked up and a man's voice answered. 'Hello.'

'Hey, Andie. It's Alex MacKay.' Alex forced his thoughts back into order. Not easy when the source of his distraction sat right beside him. But he had questions for the leader of the Sydney-based Aboriginal artist group. He had questions about the way he felt towards Jayne, too, but those had to wait. Alex wasn't sure he wanted to consider them at all anyway. 'Would your group be interested in some expansion? I won't know for sure for a week or two, but possibly creating individual items bearing certain native animals on them, or items themed to the language meaning of a township within your tribal area?'

The man was interested and the call ended on a positive note.

Alex glanced at Jayne. She'd packed up her laptop and was staring out of the window.

Now she turned and smiled and said in her low, lovely voice, 'We've been steadily climbing into mountain country.'

He followed her gaze to look at the changing scenery outside the bus's windows. As he leaned closer, the bus left the sealed road and turned onto a thinner gravel one.

'Now we descend into the valley.' Jayne sucked in a breath. 'Hairpin turns on narrow dirt roads aren't my first choice for relaxing travel, particularly in a bus and when I have no...'

'Control of the wheel?' Though she'd stopped herself from saying it, the rest of the sentence had been written all over her. He laughed before he could consider his reaction, and then had to admit to the affinity he felt for her attitude. 'I do some hair-raising things sometimes, but I only ever worry if I'm not the person in charge.'

Jayne laughed and some of her tension left her. 'I

hadn't realised it, but I think you may have guessed right about me. I do prefer to have control in certain situations.'

'The driver seems experienced and sensible.' Alex pointed to the view out of the windows. 'And there's something amazing about looking down on a canopy of tree tops, don't you think?'

'Yes. I love the fern trees mixed amongst the gum trees and other foliage.' Jayne smiled and the rest of her tension disappeared. 'And I love the scent of this kind of area. I can't wait to get off the bus and take a really deep breath. In the meanwhile, you're right. I can trust the driver. He knows what he's doing.'

When they arrived, the tour guide got to his feet. 'Let's get some fresh air.' He got off the bus quickly, leaving the driver to wait for everyone to disembark, and was soon talking to one of the resort's outdoor staff.

Once everyone had exited the bus and the driver had moved it away to find a parking bay, the tour guide called for their attention.

The guide did look as though he perhaps hadn't been sleeping well, or felt a little rundown overall. Though Jayne had wondered about his sobriety briefly yesterday, she'd made sure she got a chance to speak with him after she'd discussed that with Alex and she hadn't been able to smell even a whiff of alcohol on the man.

'If there's anyone in the group who is trained to abseil, the big rock is open for it today.' The guide pointed to what, to Jayne, looked to be a quite enormous perpendicular rock face some distance to their left.

The man explained that people could do a trail walk to reach the base where the abseilers would end their descent. 'Even as observers, you might find it interesting.'

'I wonder—' Jayne forgot what she'd been going to say. The thoughts disappeared as she turned to Alex.

She caught an expression of adrenalin and wistfulness on his face before he pushed both aside.

'You'll want to see the caves,' he said. 'This tour isn't geared to extreme sport junkies so the abseil isn't really relevant.'

'But you like extreme sports.' And, despite his efforts to conceal it, Jayne could see that he'd like to do this event.

She wanted to see him pit his strength and abilities against nature. It would be exciting. Again, Jayne was forced to acknowledge her attraction to Alex's vitality.

'There's time for both activities.' She took care to make sure her voice held nothing but neutral encouragement. 'This trip doesn't have to be entirely about work.'

'I don't want to abandon you for hours.' Alex's words were sincere, but his eyes glittered with anticipation. 'We're supposed to be info gathering.'

'Technically, *I'm* supposed to be doing that.' Though Jayne was enjoying his enthusiasm and interest in that research.

Was there anything she wasn't enjoying about Alex?

Enjoying too much!

'I'll do the walk.' Nice. Very ordinary. *Now, keep going, Jayne.* 'I'll be able to see your descent and I can talk to people at the same time.'

There. And, just in case he wasn't convinced enough, she bounced a little on the balls of her feet. 'To be honest, I miss it if I don't get some kind of exercise most days, so that'll be nice for me.'

Because, obviously, she would expire from lack of fitness if she missed more than a few days, as women of her age and above were bound to do because they were practically on their last legs physically. Jayne shoved back a frustrated frown. She wasn't *that* old.

You're not that young, either. Ten years, Jayne. And don't pretend that the fact he's younger doesn't add excitement to being aware of him as a man, because you know it does.

It also made Jayne even more uncertain of herself and her ground with him than she would be with another George or Drew or...

But Alex wasn't a George or a Drew. There was no comparison, was there?

And Alex is free. You heard him say that. So were George and Drew, but...irrelevant...

'All that running up and down stairs.' Just as Jayne had been about to start feeling depressed about her less than total youthfulness, Alex spoke. His eyes shifted over her body before they came back to rest on her face. 'I don't think you're at any risk of becoming unfit, Jayne. You're very...trim.'

'Th...thank you.' With just those few words, he

tempted her away from her reality check, made her want to think she could be as young as she wanted, was as fit as she felt and would stay that way for ever.

With Alex's admiring gaze on her, Jayne was way too aware of every curve, too aware of the wish to press those curves to the hard planes of his body, to press close and experience the intimacy of his touch as his lips lowered to hers. Too aware that she wouldn't be encroaching on another woman's territory if she explored her interest in Alex.

He wouldn't be encroaching, either. The men in Jayne's life knew she wouldn't commit to them.

She wouldn't commit to Alex either, of course.

Oh, Jayne didn't even know what she was thinking about!

'You should…' She blinked and the world around them came back into focus. People from the tour deciding what activity to do first, the scent of gum trees and loamy soil and the sounds of nature around them. Jayne drew a breath. 'You should give yourself this treat.'

'All right. You've convinced me. Thanks, Jayne. It's generous of you.' Alex took her at her word and made his way to sign up for the abseiling group.

Jayne joined the group who would meet up with the abseilers later. Maybe some time apart from Alex would help her get her thoughts back into perspective—i.e. focused on the purpose of this trip!

Three-quarters of the way to the abseil landing destination some time later, Jayne was forced to admit that plan hadn't exactly worked out.

'He's not my boyfriend. We're just touring together for…um…for other reasons.' Jayne considered increasing her walking pace to try to get away from this line of questioning, but she doubted it would help.

A couple of the university students on tour to practise their Japanese language skills had apparently also decided to practise their detective skills on Jayne's relationship with her companion. And they didn't seem to mind how blunt their questions were!

'Oh, look ahead. There's where the abseil will end.' Jayne's feeling of relief faded a little when her glance travelled upwards to the top of the mountainous area. Up and up. And up even more.

Alex was a gorgeous man. Fit and muscled and with the edge of an adrenalin-seeker that did attract Jayne. But he was going to rappel down *that*?

Hanging only from a flimsy bit of rope and a harness?

All the way to the bottom?

'Will he be safe? What if something goes wrong? I hope he knows—' She stopped herself before more words could come out.

Fortunately, the university students had moved on and were now very earnestly in discussion with several other tourists who'd also walked the trail to watch the abseiling, so at least Jayne's concerns had gone undetected.

And at least the students had given up on nosing around into Jayne's relationship with Alex. Jayne had found one of them in particular watching her more often than she would like, but perhaps he was just a little curious.

The group were to wait in a beautiful clearing of soft, low natural grasses surrounded by rock face on one side and lush trees and bushes on the other three sides. There were picnic tables but Jayne opted to stay on her feet. She could see movement at the top of the rock face and got out her camera and adjusted the lens to zoom onto that activity.

There was Alex, harnessed up and looking ready to go. Jayne sucked in a breath for two reasons as he positioned himself and then went over the edge of the drop.

In those first moments, his facial muscles tightened with anticipation, the thrill of the challenge, the thrill of letting himself fall into nothing but space. He looked thrilling to Jayne.

As he began to rappel down the rock face, all of his concentration was on the task. With a glance either side of him, he noted the positions of the others and then he gave himself to enjoying his descent.

'He needs to feel the freedom of this and the challenge of pitting himself against nature.' Jayne murmured the words and eased her death grip on the camera.

When Alex reached ground level some distance away and started to disengage from the harnessing equipment, she made her way to his side.

He glanced over his shoulder and grinned. 'That was a rush.'

'And you loved it.' Jayne smiled. 'I was a bit worried

for you at first, but then I relaxed. I could see you knew what you were doing.'

'I've abseiled before. Skydiving, too. Rock-climbing, trail bike riding, white water rafting.' Alex's face sobered. 'I don't have to have the kind of challenge of jumping off a sheer rock face. I just enjoy it as a leisure activity.'

He sounded almost defensive and Jayne didn't quite know what to say.

'It's not wrong to need certain kinds of satisfaction out of life. There wouldn't be anything out of place in you needing the thrill of extreme sports or other things like that, even if you did.' She couldn't tell him how appealing she found it. How it added to her attraction to him to know that he could pursue and conquer these kinds of activities. Jayne was struggling enough to try to control those thoughts. If they wanted to talk about what was 'wrong', it was more likely Jayne's attraction to him pushing those boundaries!

For a moment he simply looked at her before his gaze softened. 'I hadn't really looked at it that way. Well, we promised ourselves a tour through at least one cave.' He gestured with his hand. 'Maybe we should head back, see what tours we can get into before the day ends.'

'Yes. Let's do that.' As they stepped towards each other, both stilled. She'd been trying so hard, but now it all rushed to the surface again. Longing for this man, to be closer, to know him more deeply, welled once more inside her.

Alex's facial muscles tightened into a different kind

of expression. To a stillness that was about a man and a woman standing close together in a lush green valley, and wanting to stand even closer. To touch? Kiss?

As though she had leaped into thin air, Jayne's breath caught in her throat. All she could do was look into his face, see every strong feature, the creases at the outsides of his eyes, the ones on either side of his mouth that deepened when he smiled.

Alex shook his head as though to try to clear it, and Jayne blinked her eyes and tried to pull her thoughts together, too, and they moved back up the trail. She remonstrated with herself along the way.

She was in the middle of work on a challenging business proposal to put to her father. Maybe a lot of people would be satisfied with the fulfilment of the job she already had, but Jayne had earned her partnership. She was being generous, working on another proposal to put to her father, considering he'd allowed Eric to undermine Jayne's achievements on the past two.

It was time for Jayne's father to hand her the partnership, or for Jayne to leave the family company to find career fulfilment elsewhere.

'Two of the tours start within ten minutes of each other.' Alex gestured to the noticeboards outside the tourist information booth. A hint of mischief laced his tone. 'The first one has "snuggling spaces". That could be fun.'

Jayne peered at the description while one flirty response after another paraded through her head.

Don't say them, Jayne.

'It says "snug" spaces.' She tried to sound prim, and hoped she didn't sound as willing to explore the concept of snuggling in spaces with him as she was!

Her phone rang.

'I wasn't sure there'd even be reception here.' She stared at the caller ID blankly for a moment before the information registered. 'It's my sister.'

'Take the call. I'll get our tickets for the cosy tour.' With his cheeky grin once again in place, he moved off.

'Hi, Nickie.' Jayne forced the words out with determined good cheer. 'How are you? How's Cora? Is everything all right?'

Jayne had texted her sister and told her she'd be out of town until the weekend, but not that she was touring, or why.

'We're both fine. Cora still thinks kitchens are made for her to pull everything out of the cupboards and play with it.' Her sister's voice wasn't its usual cheerful tone, though it was clear she was trying.

Nickie was eight years younger than Jayne. Because of that age difference and the abandonment by their mother so many years ago, part of Jayne's bond with Nickie was almost motherly.

Nickie's tone right now worried Jayne, but Jayne tried to sound ordinary and cheerful when she replied. 'Who needs toys when there are saucepans?'

'Exactly.' Nickie drew a breath. 'Jayne, I went in to your work building today. My shift at the beauty shop started later and I'd already dropped Cora at day-care.

I had some hand cream samples I wanted to give to the reception girls. I was going to say hi to Dad while I was there so I went up to his floor.' The strain in Nickie's voice became more apparent.

And some of Jayne's pleasure in her surroundings, in this trip, became subjugated to a feeling of unease. 'What happened, Nickie?'

'Eric came along while I was waiting for Dad. He'd been out to lunch with some business people, I think, and he'd had a couple of drinks. Well, I suspect more than a couple.' Nickie drew a breath. 'So he was chatty. Jayne, he told me that while you're out of the office this week and your office space is being made over, Eric's going to be getting the larger front part of it and they're putting you at the back.'

Jayne had known Eric was influencing her father with his flattery and so on, but this…

'Jayne? Have I done the wrong thing, telling you?' Nickie's worried voice came over the line. 'I didn't want to bring it up but I didn't want you to go back to work not knowing.'

'You did the right thing.' Jayne had talked to Nickie enough times about work. 'And you don't need to worry about this, Nickie. I'll sort it out.'

'Jayney, I'm sorry that Dad doesn't respect all your hard work enough. I think you deserve that partnership, not to be treated like this.' Nickie sounded as though she wanted to burst into tears.

'Thanks, and you're right. I do deserve the partnership. Dad knows that as well. He was supposed to give it to me after the last project.' Jayne had to clear her throat. That stupid frog was back again, but for a different reason this time. 'I'll take care of this.' And she would. That was what this week was about. She would gather information and add it to the rest of her research, and pull it all together into a package deal that her father would be completely crazy to ignore.

The work Jayne put in would get her over the line to that coveted partnership. If not, she'd be leaving the company.

Jayne reassured her sister, thanked her again for calling and said goodbye.

'Is everything okay, Jayne?' Alex's words weren't intrusive, but they did express concern.

Jayne ironed the frown from her brow. 'A small problem at work.'

'Is there anything I can do to help?'

'Let's make our way to our cave tour.' Jayne made a start towards the entrance area of the first tour. She needed just a moment to collect herself because, ridiculously, his words and the care behind them had brought a prickle of emotion to the backs of her eyes. She didn't want him to see it.

'My office space is being refurbished this week. That's why I have the week off. My sister rang to let me know that some of my office space is being given to another employee.' Jayne was annoyed and more than a little offended by that fact. But she tipped up her chin and simply said, 'It's no big deal. I'll sort it out. That's a policy of mine. If some minor irritation happens at work, I try to find a way to turn the annoyance into positive forward movement of some kind.'

'I admire you for that attitude. It shows a lot of maturity.'

Did he think of her as old? The thought crept into Jayne's mind. She'd been trying to ignore it, but Alex was gorgeous and fit in a way only a man of his age could be.

And Jayne was conscious that certain parts of her were not twenty-five any more. She had wrinkles. And other less than completely attractive things that came with maturing.

They reached the waiting area for their tour and Alex glanced at his watch. 'The tour won't start for a few more minutes. Did you want to phone your office now and do something about the renovation confusion?'

'Yes, I think I will.' Jayne moved aside to make the call, and to try to pull her thoughts together. She'd allowed them to wander ridiculously, thinking about her age and wrinkles, for goodness' sake.

She dialled the number for her father's personal assistant. 'Hi, Macey. Put me through to my father, please.'

'Sure. One moment.'

'Jayne.' Her father's voice came over the line. He was neither overtly welcoming, nor unwelcoming. Just Dad. Focused on business, and on himself, mostly. 'What are you doing, phoning in? You have the week off.'

'I'm phoning about my office space. I don't want it rearranged. I worked hard for my front space and I'm not prepared to give it up to Eric. I am in a more senior position than him.' There was no point trying to be subtle about it.

'Well, now, Jayne—' her father's voice took on a blustering tone '—Eric has pointed out that he really could do with more space than he has currently.'

'Regardless, I have quite a few years of seniority on him and I'm not prepared to give him that workspace, so please make sure that's taken care of.' Jayne sucked in one short breath of air. 'And I'd like a meeting with you first thing Monday morning when I come back into the office. I'll have something quite exciting to put to you.'

'All right.' Her father sighed. 'I could do with some good news.'

And of course he would want that because he didn't cope well when he was on his own, and his fifth marriage had broken up recently. Why couldn't he allow his daughters to bring personal fulfilment, find more joy in them, instead of allowing them in to a certain degree but no further?

'You'll sort things out about my office space?'

There was silence for a moment. 'I suppose I could find Eric another large office area and give it to him solely.'

This wasn't quite the response Jayne had looked for, but at least her space would be left alone. 'I'll speak with you Monday, Dad. Goodbye for now.'

Jayne had intended to wait a few days before booking the meeting, but it seemed smarter to do it now.

Her father said his abrupt goodbye and hung up. At least that issue was taken care of.

Jayne made her way back to Alex. 'Let's tackle this cave tour.'

A cosy tour through lots of confined spaces.

To keep an eye open for pillow gift ideas and nothing else! Jayne reminded herself.

CHAPTER FIVE

'DINNER was lovely. This resort really does have its charm.' Jayne looked across the table towards Alex.

He had his charm, too. Charm and a good dose of thoughtfulness to go with the streak of good humour that was just as much a part of him.

He'd been the one to cheekily suggest the snug cave tour, and they'd viewed both caves. The first had indeed been *snug*.

Enough that Jayne had become a little too claustrophobic in there a couple of times. Alex had caught her trapped expression very quickly. He'd taken her hand and tucked it securely into his and started in on 'cave' jokes until she'd been quietly giggling so much she'd forgotten to feel trapped.

Jayne—giggling—as a mature businesswoman!

Somehow she had felt both secure at his side and very conscious of him all at once as his fingers had stroked gently over hers and he told his silly jokes.

By the time they'd emerged from the second cave, Jayne had decided that 'underground' was not her most favourite place of all, but Alex had got her through the tours beautifully and by then night had fallen. The resort looked gorgeous with stars twinkling in the sky and its backdrop of mountains. And she now felt wonderfully relaxed and content.

'I think I've let myself fall into holiday mode.' She blamed those feelings on that, but in truth she was content in Alex's company. Jayne had let down some of her guard with him today.

Be careful about letting him in, Jayne.

'It's okay to relax sometimes.' Alex's gaze held hers and seemed to say more. Perhaps that he'd relaxed with her as well, and liked her company. 'I've enjoyed the time with you.'

'I guess cave formations as a background for those travel clocks might do for this tour.' Right at this moment, Jayne didn't care as much about all of that as she should. She simply wanted to sit here, to look into his eyes. There was an intimacy in her feelings that was dangerous, and yet Jayne couldn't seem to shake loose of this state of mind. 'Or maybe something more exciting will come to light in the first half of tomorrow, before we hop on that plane to join up with the outback tour group.'

Jayne looked into Alex's eyes and felt she'd already found that excitement…in him.

'You've relaxed after your phone calls.' Alex sat back as the waitress brought their coffees and, when she'd left, went on, 'I'm glad about that.'

He seemed relaxed, too. But a different kind of tension was there in his eyes, in the softness of his mouth as he looked at her and in his body language as he leaned forward once again and propped his elbows on the table as he gave her all of his attention.

'I hope this trip will be worthwhile for you, Alex.' He'd said he had other dealings along the way.

'I'm hoping the research in Alice Springs will be. I've been told I have biological history there.' He drew a breath and seemed surprised that he had confided this. 'If I do have family in the area, I want to meet them.'

He'd said he'd grown up in an orphanage. 'If there's anything I can do to help you with that—'

'Thanks.' His mouth turned up at the corners. 'Cross your fingers is about all.'

She returned his smile. 'Will you be okay, trying to trace biological family while on our tour?' Jayne wanted to support that effort. 'My mother is lost to me but that's different. She was part of my life for the first fifteen years. You can have as much time as you need.'

'I need to speak to some of the tribal elders there.' Alex took a sip of his coffee and his attention seemed to focus inwardly before he went on. 'Even if they can't help me discover who my father was, they may at least be able to help me understand the part of my make-up that is Aboriginal. I grew up and into manhood without knowing about that. I do feel the need to know where I've come from.'

'I went through a lot of loss when Mum left.' Jayne hadn't meant to admit the words, but they made their way out. 'She walked out on the whole family, not just Dad. She left and I never heard from her again. None of

us did. I couldn't understand how she could do that—
leave her children like that.'

His hand closed over hers where it rested on the table.
Strong fingers wrapped around her slender ones as his
gaze held hers. 'The choices people make are sometimes
impossible to explain.'

He was right, and it was a conclusion Jayne had eventually come to. There'd just been a lot of soul-searching
as a teen, feeling her loss and wondering if it was her
fault somehow, until she'd turned all of her focus to her
work because at least that got her away from the rest of
it. Helped her to stay a step removed from her mother
leaving and her father starting on his trail of young
brides. And Nickie, getting hurt, too, when she became
pregnant and the father of her baby didn't want to stick
around.

'How does someone your age have the amount of
wisdom that you do, Alex? To know when the only
choice is to accept something, whether deep down you
can accept it or even understand it?' Jayne was a decade
older than Alex and yet he seemed to match her perhaps
in that maturity that came with life experience that he'd
first mentioned when she'd brought up his age.

It was hard to remember he was so young.

*You need to remember it, Jayne, otherwise you're no
better than your father. Maybe thinking about that will
help you stay right away from thoughts about wearing
spotted clothes!*

'I don't know that I'd say I have any special degree
of wisdom.' Alex's hand still held hers, but shadows

came into his eyes as he went on. 'Ambition, having goals, being determined to have certain things, those I know. They're what have made me work harder at understanding the world. So I can utilise it to help me meet my goals. I'm not sure they'll be a lot of help in my search for my history.'

'You mentioned you grew up with brothers.'

'Yes.' He nodded. 'We're not biologically related. We were all in the orphanage together. I think we're tighter than a lot of related siblings. Maybe because we chose the relationship.' He shook his head. 'I'm surprised I unloaded all that on you. I haven't spoken to my brothers about my research yet.' A smile softened the corners of his mouth. 'I guess you're easy to talk to, Jayne.'

Jayne felt flattered. At the same time, she felt an affinity for Alex, a trust in him that she didn't normally give easily. It was why she'd opened up about her own family situation, too.

As she watched, he visibly pushed his thoughts aside. 'And you, Jayne? Is it just the one sister, and your father?'

'And my niece, Cora, yes. Nickie was seven years old when Mum left.'

'And you pretty much raised her from then?' How had he guessed? Maybe because of all Jayne hadn't said about that? Her father hadn't remarried for five years and, even then, his new wife was never going to be mother material for Nickie.

Jayne hadn't been, either, but she'd been Nickie's sister. 'I wish I could have shielded her more. She had some unhappy times.' Nickie had moved away for over a year, fallen pregnant in that time and had kept making excuses for not wanting to let Jayne visit her. She'd come home with a little baby and needing support from her family. Dad had treated the whole thing as though it was not his problem and left Jayne to worry about picking up the pieces.

At least Jayne had been able to give Nickie her support. 'She seems content with Cora and her job in the beauty shop now.'

'I think you have more wisdom than you credit yourself with, Jayne.' His fingers tightened against hers and he met her gaze very directly.

Jayne looked into Alex's eyes. He didn't know what she would see. He couldn't believe how easy it had been to open up to her, how much he had enjoyed getting to know her better. Being with Jayne somehow helped to ease the restlessness inside him that had been a problem all his life. He didn't understand how or why, but it did.

He'd abseiled today, and he'd enjoyed it. Usually he went after activities like that to give him an outlet for his restless feelings. Today he would have been just as happy to enjoy Jayne's company anywhere, doing anything. Images of certain things they could do together surfaced, and Alex pushed them back. That was his other problem—an attraction to Jayne that strengthened with each passing moment. And that had deepened even more as he'd got to know her this evening.

Jayne drew her hand from his and tucked it beneath

the table. He felt the loss of her touch, and he felt the warmth that remained in his palm and fingers where they'd held her.

The waiter came to their table then and asked if they'd like anything else and Jayne declined and got to her feet.

Alex stood with her, and they made their way out of the restaurant. He walked with her up the flight of stairs and to the door of her room. The corridor was quiet, deserted. As they paused outside her door, Jayne cast a helpless glance his way.

That glance held all of her confusion and the closeness they'd gained from talking over dinner, and consciousness and awareness and interest.

'I don't know what I want.' She whispered it.

He nodded because he understood, and he knew what he should want and that he could end up out of his depth with her too easily. He was already halfway there. But they both wanted this.

His fingers lightly brushed against the back of her hand and she leaned towards him, leaned into that small touch as though she craved more.

'Jayne.' He tipped up her chin with his hand.

Alex let his eyelids drift down as he leaned closer until their lips gently brushed and he got the first taste of her, the first heady sensation of kissing her, of feeling her lips soften and yield beneath his.

Kissing Jayne was unlike any kiss Alex had shared before. And when she opened her mouth and yielded even more deeply to what they were sharing, Alex's arms closed around her and he held her and, somewhere inside him, he registered the preciousness of Jayne and of this moment, even if he didn't fully understand his feelings.

Jayne kissed Alex and her hands rose to his strong forearms and found their way to his shoulders and around his neck and she pressed close to him and couldn't get enough—of firm lips sipping at hers, pressing to hers, plying her mouth and filling her with the taste of him.

His body was firm everywhere, muscled and fit, lean and youthful. The last thought should have made Jayne hesitate but it didn't. She focused on this moment and set all other thoughts aside and kissed him. Hungrily kissed him. Ravenously kissed him. Kissed him as though she never ever wanted to stop.

Her senses stirred. Desire stirred. And, deep inside, other parts of her unfurled, wanted to trust him, to believe in the possibility of a relationship and closeness with him.

Not like the associations she had with the casual dates in her life. More than that. Commitment.

Jayne's fingers stilled against the sides of his neck. A little well of panic rose. Alex—gorgeous, young, attractive Alex—

What made her think she could pull off commitment with him? Emotional commitment, because that was what she held back from her male friends. What made her think, if she could take on something like that, that he would want it, anyway?

'I can't. This mustn't...' Jayne broke away from his

kiss, from strong arms that had made her feel safe. Alex
was a good man. He had a good work ethic and Jayne
hoped theirs would be a great ongoing working relationship. But they couldn't have anything else. A sense of
panic washed through her. She couldn't have anything
else. Not with Alex.

Because he's younger. It wouldn't be appropriate.

Yes. That was the reason. Jayne accepted it with
almost a sense of relief. Jayne didn't want to be caught
looking foolish.

*It's not because in thirty-five years you've never
trusted enough in a relationship to allow strong feelings to develop and now you're scared Alex might bring
these feelings out in you because you've reacted more
to him in a single day than you have to the string of
Georges and Drews who've shifted through your life for
years?*

Jayne's only relationship success story was Nickie
and, during the time that her sister had moved away,
Jayne had not been a success there, either.

'It's late.' Actually, it wasn't that late but the words
were all Jayne could come up with. 'I should turn in.'

'Jayne.' Alex's hands dropped away from her and
came to rest loosely at his sides. He looked as though
he might have been going to say something, Jayne didn't
know what.

In that moment she felt as old as she was, conscious
of every year that had passed, and there was Alex, in
the prime of his twenties, attractive and young and

with more of life ahead of him and every choice open to him.

'I have my dating arrangements,' she blurted. 'Two men who I see who meet those social needs, and some other occasional dates. My career—I'm not looking to settle down.'

It was the truth, in its way, but none of it was all of Jayne's truth about this issue. She wasn't sure she'd ever allowed herself to really examine 'her' truths about relationships, commitment and so on.

Well, that was because half of all that was pure fairy tale. Nice to imagine, but highly unlikely to ever happen. Dad, and her mother, and Nickie, were all proof of that, as was Jayne's inability to find anyone she wanted to do more than go out with here and there.

Jayne hastened to add, 'Not that I'm suggesting you were looking for a relationship.'

'It's okay, Jayne. This—' he gestured with one hand before that hand returned to his side and his expression was unreadable, guarded, as he continued '—it probably shouldn't have happened. I'm not looking for anything serious either, and I have other issues on my mind during this trip as well.'

'It might be best if we just treated this as though it hadn't happened.'

Alex agreed, and they said goodnight. Jayne retired to her room, worked on her proposal for a few hours and went to bed.

If her thoughts strayed to Alex, to a kiss she had wanted, which had brought feelings out in her that she didn't want to acknowledge, she told herself that stopping that kiss, making sure it wouldn't be repeated, had been in the best interests of both of them. It had been the sensible thing to do.

And Alex didn't want commitment, either. He'd just said so. Which meant she had, indeed, done the right thing just now.

Sensible, staid, *not at all interested in following a path of women showing interest in younger men,* Jayne put herself to bed. She didn't feel even slightly depressed. Or leopard-printish about life.

CHAPTER SIX

ALEX woke after a restless night's sleep. It was no surprise that his first thought was of Jayne. He forced his body out of bed and showered.

Once he'd dressed, he picked up his phone and called his brother, Linc. As the phone rang, thoughts of Jayne finally pushed further through his mind.

She had thrown herself into their kiss, and then quickly retreated. She'd seemed a little overwhelmed by what they had shared. Had she rejected their kiss, warned him off for that reason?

He hadn't liked hearing about those other men she was seeing but, in the light of a new day, her attitude seemed to confirm what he'd thought when she'd taken that phone call from one of them. She wasn't attached.

The problem was that Alex had never sought a deep attachment with a woman. Yet he'd felt as though he needed that kiss last night with Jayne, from some place deep inside him. He did feel possessive about Jayne, even though logic told him that was a ridiculous way to feel. Those were the things that Alex couldn't figure out.

'Hello, little brother. How are you doing on your bus tour?'

'Hey, Linc. It's going okay. How are you? Have you sunk my business yet?' Alex tried hard for a cheerful, good-humoured tone of teasing. He'd been trying hard for that with Linc and Brent for five weeks now.

Oh, they both knew something was up. Brent had pinned him down three weeks ago, told him if there was trouble to spit it out so they could help him deal with it. Alex had said he was fine, but this was something he was going to have to discuss eventually.

'I've been trying, but it's resisting my efforts to bring it undone.' Linc dropped the jocular tone and gave a quick rundown. 'You know your people are fine when you're not there. I'm just around in case there are any actual dramas, in which case I'd contact you anyway.'

'Yup. Works well, doesn't it?' Alex nodded, even though he knew Linc couldn't see him doing it.

'It does. Hold on a sec, Alex.'

'Sure.' Alex heard a woman's voice, a short exchange of words. And, when Linc came back on the line, a certain edge in his brother's tone that hadn't been there a moment earlier.

'Your staff don't need me around,' Linc said. 'They know what they're doing, though I'm always more than willing to make myself available to them.'

Which meant Alex could leave Sydney from time to time with peace of mind. 'I know and I appreciate it. Was that the lovely Cecilia you were speaking to just now?'

'Yeah. She's a good plant nursery manager,' Linc growled. 'If I could just get it through her head that I'm not trying to take over when—'

'—you're there and you take over. I know.' Alex had just started grinning when his brother spoke again.

'How are things going for you with Jayne Cutter? You sounded as though this deal possibility had hit you right between the eyes the last time we talked.'

'Fine. It's going fine.' *Kissing Jayne had been quite fine. More than fine.* As for what was ahead, his research in Alice Springs— 'Linc, I need to tell—'

'Hey, Alex. Would you mind if I let you go?' Linc sounded distracted. 'I can hear Cecilia on the nursery's phone. It sounds as though there might be a problem. I'd better be on hand to help with it.'

'Sure.' It wasn't relief that Alex felt. He would tell Linc, and Brent, about his situation. That would just have to wait a little longer.

Maybe it would be best to hold back on that discussion until after he did his research in Alice Springs, anyway. That way, he'd be able to share any answers he found at the same time. 'Bye, Linc. I'll call you again when I have time.'

Alex glanced at his watch and scooped up his room key. Maybe, once he saw Jayne face to face, he would settle down about last night's kiss, too. He'd probably blown it out of proportion in his memory.

Jayne was at a dining table, trying to absorb the news

she'd just received, when Alex came to join her. She offered a quiet greeting.

'Morning, Jayne.' Alex searched her face and frowned. 'What's going on?'

That quickly, he worked out there was a problem and straight away Jayne confided in him.

'The tour guide, John, is quite sick.' She uttered the words in an undertone while people around them sat at their dining tables eating the buffet of breakfast cereals and sausages and ham and eggs with toast, and sipping hot tea and coffee and orange juice. Well, she had to tell Alex. This wasn't something she could keep from him. 'It's his gall bladder.'

Jayne felt a little ill herself, but that was the result of having the bus driver come and dump this news on her. 'John's been taken to the hospital and he is going to be fine, but he's got to have an operation and he'll be laid up for some time after it.'

'Which leaves the tour without a bilingual guide until another one can be brought in.' Alex frowned.

'Yes. And that won't happen before well into this afternoon. The company can't get anyone faster than that.'

Jayne and Alex were supposed to bus out of the resort area this morning, then leave this tour and catch a flight to Alice Springs at lunchtime.

'While I was waiting for you,' Jayne went on, 'the driver came to me and broke the news about John getting sick. They both knew from the start that I was a

Cutter.' Jayne hadn't been thrilled to hear that. 'They recognised me from company photos, apparently.'

'And the driver told you there's a need for a bilingual guide to cover today, otherwise he has to try to manage by himself? Is that even allowed?'

'It's not on. There has to be a guide as well as the driver for our tours,' Jayne murmured and fought with herself because her mind and her thoughts wanted to go in too many directions at once.

Don't think about kissing Alex!

But it was all she could think of, with his closeness making her so aware of him.

'Will you do it?' Alex asked in a quiet voice.

For a moment Jayne thought he was asking if she'd kiss him again. The *yes* that rose in her thoughts was instant, despite what she'd said to the contrary after their kiss. What did Alex think about last night? Had he half forgotten it already? Had he been quite comfortable with Jayne's withdrawal? Had he perhaps been relieved, hoping she wouldn't take one insignificant kiss and want to pursue him as a result of it?

The tour, Jayne!

She had to guide the tour today. 'I've never been in charge of a tour group, but I can't leave them in the lurch. I can speak Japanese and I'm employed by the company. I'm the best bet they have.'

There. Her thoughts were where they needed to be. Still in 'nervous central' but because of work, not thanks to confusion about what she wanted with Alex MacKay. Jayne knew what she wanted—to work with him and keep any other complications out of it. That simply had to be what she wanted.

Jayne sucked in a breath. 'Maybe you should go on ahead without me to join the next tour.'

But he shook his head. 'I won't leave you to do this by yourself. My research will still be there, whether I lose half a day with this tour or not. I haven't finalised any appointments yet. In truth, I'd hoped if I didn't give too much notice I might have a better chance of people being prepared to see me during the brief time I'll be in the area.'

Jayne hoped so. As for today and the tour: 'Thanks, Alex. I'd rather do this with at least one familiar face sitting in the crowd.'

'You can do it, Jayne. You've spoken with most of the group already. It will mean blowing your cover, but a brief explanation and reassurance to them will make all the difference to how you're received. And it'll only be for today.' The faith in his eyes told her he knew she could succeed.

Jayne knew it too, but having that kind of confidence handed to her without question, without reserve and so generously as he set his own goals back moved her. 'How can you be sure I'm able—?'

'I know you, Jayne.' He said it as though it were a given, as though that feeling of knowing was not strange at all. 'Tell the driver you'll do it. You'll probably need time to talk to him, to see what he can let you know about today's itinerary.'

Alex gestured to the food on the table. 'Once we've

eaten, I'll pack for myself and for you, too, if you want, then bring our things down.'

'I'm packed, but bringing the luggage down would help.' Offering to do that for her while she spoke again to the driver almost felt like something a boyfriend would do. But all they'd done was share a kiss.

A stunning kiss.

'You know you don't need to worry about…last night.' His low words drew her from her reverie, made her aware that expressions must have been chasing each other across her face.

How did he feel about their kiss?

Alex probably regretted it and wanted to focus on their working relationship. Maybe he felt Jayne had instigated it, practically pushed herself on him? Maybe their kiss had been…a disappointment to him?

'You're a lot younger than me,' she blurted. 'Also, if you didn't really want—'

'I wanted.' His gaze held hers and refused to let go. 'And so what about my age? That kind of gap is irrelevant, anyway.'

'You'd think my father believes so.' Jayne stopped, then rushed on again. 'I don't want to get too involved with a man. What happened last night—I'm not suggesting it made you want to get particularly involved. You said otherwise and you've probably put it behind you by now, anyway. But I should have respected our working relationship and made sure it didn't happen in the first place.'

A frown came over Alex's face.

Whatever he might have said was lost when the bus driver approached their table with an apologetic expression. 'Forgive the intrusion, but could I have a word with you, Jayne?'

Jayne cast one torn glance in Alex's direction, but he just gestured to the empty seat beside him and invited the driver to sit in it.

What else could Jayne do? She'd said her piece. They would just get on with things now, get to the end of these few days of touring. Jayne would put her proposal to her father and, when it went ahead, she might have some contact with Alex here and there in relation to the supply of gifts.

This was the clean-cut arrangement that would best serve both their business interests. Jayne told herself she was resolved now. She had everything worked out as it needed to be. She could relax on the topic.

So why didn't she feel relaxed?

'Good morning, everyone. I hope you all slept well and are ready for today's tour events.' Jayne spoke the words in a calm, confident tone and repeated them in Japanese.

She stood at the front of the bus with a pleasant, cheerful expression on her face. Totally handling this, and doing it with style. Jayne was amazing, even if the thought of getting personally involved with him obviously scared her. Well, it had just been a kiss, Alex reminded himself. No big deal. He could let it go. Of course he could. He didn't want any complications, either, after all.

And Jayne. Here and now—

She could have turned her back on the group, could have said they'd just have to wait until later today when a new guide could get here.

Instead, Jayne had stepped up to the challenge. Alex could see the hint of nerves she was keeping in check. And, when she briefly caught his eye, he let her see his approval because he hoped it would encourage her.

Jayne seemed to fully relax then. She drew a breath and briefly explained who she was and why she'd taken on the job of tour guide today.

'I think you'll find today will be quite exciting, so please sit back and enjoy the trip up out of the valley. The scenic views will be spectacular at this hour of the morning.

'We have two short stops. One at mid-morning and then for lunch,' Jayne went on. 'In the afternoon we're touring what is reputed to be one of Australia's leading "haunted museums" where the ghost of a famous outlaw is said to walk the halls of the old homestead. You'll have a first-hand experience of local folklore and history.'

The group settled in for the trip.

Alex forced his attention away from Jayne's beautiful voice, from the strength of her presentation and all the other things he was coming more and more to admire about her. They'd agreed it wouldn't be wise to pursue an interest in each other. Jayne didn't want that. Alex didn't want any complications either. He didn't know how to manage the kind of complication that Jayne could be.

He wasn't disappointed that they'd both agreed on that decision.

Liar.

Alex pushed the thoughts away and turned his attention to his phone. He needed to firm up his arrangements to meet certain people in Alice Springs this evening and tomorrow morning. He would focus on that.

The start of the morning passed uneventfully, but that didn't last.

'Everything is all right, and we're going to just go back over to that lovely grassy area by the bus and spend a few minutes quietly there.' Jayne gestured with one hand.

'Thank you. I would rather be away from the homestead.' The panicky tour group member nodded. The woman had been in the middle of the haunted homestead tour when she'd realised a necklace she always wore for luck was missing. Though this might seem like nothing to some people, she felt she was taking her life into her hands by being on the haunted tour without the lucky charm.

Jayne touched the woman's hand gently, doing her best to offer what reassurance she could. 'We'll ask the driver to look through the bus for your necklace. Maybe it will turn up there.'

'I'll go ahead and ask him to start looking.' With a

brief glance in Jayne's direction, Alex strode ahead to where the bus was parked.

Jayne watched him go, watched his broad shoulders moving as he ate up the distance. He'd been so supportive when this had happened, had been supportive of Jayne all morning. She'd sensed his faith in her—that had made it very easy to do a good job of guiding the tour.

By the time Jayne got to the bus with the woman, Alex and the driver had searched it.

Alex came to their sides. 'No luck there. Sorry.'

'I don't know where the necklace could be. I know I put it on this morning.'

Jayne comforted the stressed woman, helped her think through all the places the necklace might be. She got on the phone to last night's accommodation and had the staff check the woman's room and the common areas while the driver pulled out the entire luggage from the hold of the bus.

'It's not here, either.' The woman reluctantly closed the lid on her suitcase and turned to Jayne. 'I'm sorry for causing extra work, but visiting the haunted homestead without that—'

'Not at all, and I hope we'll still find your necklace.' Jayne drew a breath. 'In the meantime, is there anything that I can help you with, to ease your mind?'

Alex watched Jayne helping the distraught passenger. He had the feeling Jayne would go to any lengths to help the woman regain her confidence.

He added quietly, 'Is there any other item we can

get for you that would work in the same way as the charm?'

'Another charm, maybe, but no, thank you. I will wait and hope the necklace is found.' The woman shivered and opened her travel shoulder bag and drew out her cardigan.

As she pushed her hand into the sleeve, she paused and a look of surprise came over her face. A moment later the necklace was in her hands, and then around her neck while she beamed and looked embarrassed at once. 'I checked this. I mustn't have closed the necklace clasp properly and now it is in my sleeve! I am sorry for all the trouble.'

'It's not a problem at all.' Jayne simply smiled. 'I helped you check everything, remember? I didn't see it in there, either.'

They were able to return to the tour of the homestead then. Jayne's shoulders appeared a little tense, but otherwise she showed no sign that she had just torn a bus apart trying to find the missing item.

An hour later, the tour of the homestead and museum was over and done. The bus stopped outside the day's accommodation in a large country town which had a thriving shopping centre, cinemas, live entertainment and more. Jayne finished debriefing the newly arrived replacement tour guide and started towards Alex, where he stood beside the taxi that would take them to the airport. They had seats on the last flight out of here to Alice Springs.

As she made her way over to Alex, Mr and Mrs Li

also approached. They smiled at Jayne and Mr Li spoke. 'You have done an excellent job of taking over as tour guide, Miss Cutter. Would it be possible for you to stay in that role for the remainder of the tour?'

'Oh, that's very flattering, but I'm afraid I can't.' Jayne appeared both somewhat tired and appreciative. 'Alex and I have other commitments. In fact, we need to leave you now.' She gestured towards the taxi. 'We need to get to the airport.'

Mr Li presented his business card. 'Then I will say this briefly but trust that you understand I am completely serious in this offer.'

Jayne drew a breath. 'I don't quite understand.'

'You have a voice that would record beautifully and you speak fluent Japanese.' He went on, 'Added to this, you know the tourist industry. If you might be interested in a very lucrative business arrangement with me, I would like to speak with you about being the voice of all the virtual tour recordings I will begin marketing in Japan in the next few months.'

'You're setting up in competition to Cutter's?' Jayne's voice was quite emotionless and her expression hadn't changed. But she'd become guarded, just the same.

'No.' Mr Li shook his head. 'The tourists I bring in to the country will come due to my advertising efforts in corporations and businesses in Japan. They will come as business groups. It is unlikely that they would come otherwise. Please, if you would like to know more, give me a call and we can arrange to speak further about this.'

'Thank you. I will. I'll…call you,' Jayne said a little numbly, and they said their farewells. She and Alex climbed into the taxi.

They'd made the fifteen-minute trip to the airport, checked their luggage and boarded the small plane before Jayne turned to Alex and finally verbalised her surprise. 'Mr Li offered me a job. On the strength of my ability to speak Japanese and the sound of my voice?'

'Not quite just that.' Alex said it gently as the plane made its ascent into the sky. 'You did an amazing job today, you know. And remember Mr Li had already spent an evening talking about the tourist industry with you before today happened. And he knew who you were, which means he would have really understood your experience and expertise in tourism.'

'They said they were interested in the industry, but I had no idea. I didn't know they'd value my insights like that.' Jayne paused while the flight attendant offered refreshments. She and Alex each took a cup of coffee.

'Voicing virtual tours.' A hint of excitement crept into Jayne's voice. 'If he was prepared to pay me for that on a contractual basis and I could fit it in with the hours I work for Cutter's, it sounds as though there wouldn't be any conflict of interest in doing the work.'

'That's right.' Alex nodded and shifted slightly in the seat. His thigh brushed Jayne's and she was instantly back in her thoughts to kissing him.

But there was something else to think about that was even more important at the moment. 'Alex, did you manage to make your appointments? I really hope today's delay won't interfere with your search process.'

'I have an appointment booked for an hour after we land, and another one for tomorrow morning.'

'Good.' As they'd spoken, his shoulders had locked. Jayne wished she could hold him and let her hands stroke his tension away. She wished she could go with him to his appointments. All she could do was wish him well.

'I'll be there when you're finished. I don't mind missing some of tomorrow's tour, or all of it.'

'Thanks, Jayne. That's generous but I'm sure we'll be able to cover most of the tour tomorrow.' The descent light came on and he clipped his seat belt and waited while she did the same. 'I guess we'll just see how things go with the appointments. Now, let's cover that last tour while we have a few minutes.'

'I've settled on providing each of the guests with a charm in either the form of a necklace or bracelet. The charms would each be individually crafted to represent some aspect of the tour, and they would offer good luck.'

'Inspired by the haunted tour.' Alex smiled. 'That's a good idea.'

Pleased that he liked her thoughts, Jayne smiled. 'Can you find someone to create the charms for me?' She corrected herself, 'I mean for Cutter's?'

'Yes, I can. I have a costume jeweller working for me who'll be ideal for the work.'

'Thank you, Alex.' His contacts were working out to be as good as Jayne had hoped they would be.

He glanced out of the window. 'Won't be long until we land.' The plane started to slow.

Jayne's fingers curled around the armrest of her seat and anticipation and a little worry for him all blended together inside her. Whatever he was about to find out about his past, they were almost there!

CHAPTER SEVEN

THE evening passed slowly for Jayne. She couldn't stop thinking about Alex's meeting. Was it going okay? Was he hearing good news? Or bad?

'There you are. You're back. I didn't mean to hover in the hallway. I just stepped out for a moment.' Jayne babbled the words and stopped abruptly. 'Sorry. The last thing you probably need is me blabbing at you.' She searched Alex's face. 'How...how did things go?'

'It was a little intense.' Alex felt drained. It had been a deep and at times frustrating few hours. He was still processing the meeting with several local elders.

'I've got a suite with a separate sitting room,' Jayne offered. 'Would you like a coffee or a cold drink?'

He hesitated for a moment, but he could probably benefit from talking the meeting over a bit. It might help clarify his thoughts. 'That'd be nice.'

They sat with a bottle of soft drink each and Alex started to sift through his thoughts. 'None of the elders could place me.'

At least they'd met him, and they'd tried. 'They all met me at once, so there's no meeting now for tomorrow.'

'And this one didn't get as far as you'd hoped?' Jayne's hand closed over his where it rested on the table. 'I'm sorry, Alex. Is there more that can be done?'

Her fingers were soft and gentle, and it made Alex feel like a big baby for wanting to…hold on.

'I don't know where to take it from here. I'm usually decisive.' It would have been easy for Alex to want to bury his disappointment here, now, with Jayne. He wanted to—wanted her—and, because he already felt vulnerable, he got to his feet.

If his father's identity remained a mystery to him, he'd deal with it. 'I have an invitation from the elders to come back to Alice Springs and spend some time with them.' Alex appreciated that and one day he would probably do it. He did want to understand his history and embrace cultural aspects of himself that he hadn't done until now, even if he couldn't pin it down to more than that.

As Jayne walked with him to the door of her sitting room, she glanced up with concern on her face.

'Don't worry about it.' He touched her cheek, just once. It was all he would allow himself—one touch before he said goodnight, stepped out into the hallway and listened for her to lock the door behind him.

Alex had told Jayne not to worry but, truthfully, this had made him feel more restless inside than ever. He was…disappointed. He'd wanted to stay talking to Jayne, to soak up her concern for him. He'd wanted to kiss her again, and to…more than kiss her. Oh, he knew none of that would make any difference to his lack of answers from tonight's meeting, but he'd wanted it anyway.

Alex wasn't comfortable with the knowledge of that want. He couldn't think right now about the right or wrong of trying to pursue this with Jayne. The attraction seemed to increase as they got to know each other but they'd also both said that pursuing it was not what they truly wanted. For that reason, he chose to leave.

To walk away instead of resolving it? To ignore it instead of dealing with it? As he'd been ignoring the fact that he had to discuss his search for answers with Brent and Linc? The thoughts brought a frown to his face.

'The shadows that the clouds are casting on the rock as they move overhead almost look like spirits or something. Do you see the two faces? The hand holding a spear?' Jayne whispered the words.

Alex stood at her side. They'd come to watch the sun rise over Uluru the next morning. The huge red rock was planted in the centre of this dry, dusty plain. All around them were wiry trees and scrubby bushes, barren red earth and ripples of dust. There was an air of stillness and waiting that seemed to come from deep within the earth, not just from the people around them who held their breaths as the sun broke over the landscape.

The catch of Jayne's breath was audible. 'This is beautiful. I almost feel as though I shouldn't be here. That the sun should be allowed to rise and set undisturbed.'

'It's sacred ground. Maybe that's what you're feeling.'

Alex had felt the impact, too, the first time he'd come out here with his friend and colleague, Brendan. However you looked at it, Uluru was a place that commanded respect. He was glad Jayne had felt its strength.

Alex hadn't known, during his other visit, that he had a history in this area. Now he did, though his information about it was limited and he wasn't really sure what he wanted to do now about that heritage. He didn't know what he'd wanted in the first place, when he'd received his mother's letter.

Closure on something that he'd been forced to close many years ago because it had all been unanswerable at that time? Answers to feelings of abandonment and loss that were also unanswerable? Absolution for still feeling empty in a corner of himself, despite the care and love of Brent and Linc that should have filled any void?

'Where does seeing this put you in relation to this tour?' He'd rather ask this question of Jayne and ignore his own questions.

'I don't think this is something that the tour should capitalise on.' As the sun finally climbed fully into the sky, Jayne turned to meet his gaze. 'I know there's a lot of touristy stuff out there that does exactly that, and I wouldn't want to stop people from buying a photo or print of the rock or the area.'

'But you don't think it would be right for Cutter's to try to profit from the magic,' he suggested.

'Exactly.' Jayne searched his face before she started back to join their tour guide. 'However, it's an inspiring area and I hope we'll come up with something we can use to represent it to the people who take this tour.'

It was a different tour group, Australians mostly, from cities or other parts of the country who had not been here before. For the main part, most people had been struck silent by the majesty and aura of this area.

Jayne and Alex walked a few more metres in silence. He appreciated that she wasn't asking him further questions about his…research and situation here. Right now, he didn't feel able to answer any of them.

As his gaze shifted ahead, a slow smile spread from the corners of his eyes to his mouth. 'Look who's here.'

Jayne followed Alex's gaze to a man leaning against the side of a jeep. As she watched, the man straightened and tipped back the bushman's hat on his head. White teeth flashed.

'Is that Brendan?' Alex had filled Jayne in on who Brendan was and what he may be able to tell him. She wanted—needed—to comfort Alex, to find his answers for him, but Jayne knew from her experience with her mother that it wasn't necessarily that simple. Sometimes there were no answers, and sometimes the only comfort that could come was the passage of time. But if Alex could enjoy seeing his friend, that would be good.

'Yup. That's Brendan all right. Good of him to come out here.' Alex walked forward. The men exchanged a hand grip and slapped each other's backs.

'Hope you don't mind me coming out while you're paying your respects to the rock?' There was a hint of

teasing in Brendan's gaze, but also shrewdness in his
expression, and more understanding than there might
have been.

How much had Alex told Brendan of the purpose of
his trip here? Of his search?

Alex started to shrug, and then shook his head. 'It
moved me. It's as if that rock knows things about me.
Right now, that's not a thought that sits all that well. I
could do with some answers.'

Before Brendan could respond, Alex turned to Jayne.
'Jayne, I'd like you to meet Brendan Carroll. Brendan,
this is Jayne Cutter. You got my message about potential
interest in your work, Brendan?'

Brendan had, and he dipped his head as he said so.
'Got your message about last night's meeting, too.'

'Yeah. The outcome was disappointing. I appreciated
everyone coming out for it, though.' Alex shrugged, as
though to allay that disappointment. 'It's good to see
you. When I sent you that text last night I wasn't sure if
you'd have time to meet with us today.'

'I made time.' Brendan's words were somehow blunt,
his expression still searching before he turned to smile
at Jayne. 'It's nice to meet you.'

Jayne exchanged greetings with the other man. For
the second time since meeting Alex, Jayne then found
herself looking at amazing original artworks from
the back of a four-wheel drive. Brendan had brought
twenty samples of artworks on rock with him. Not
rock that shouldn't be taken from this area, but rock,
just the same.

'My father owns cattle country north of here. I'm stockman and artist mixed into one.' Brendan shrugged his shoulders. 'We cleared a lot of the rocks from three sections a few years ago to put some effort into getting trees in. I painted the first few rocks for doorstops for the homestead. After that, people started asking for them.'

Jayne examined the piece of rock she held in her hand. Brendan had depicted the landscape of this area in reds and oranges, black, blues, greens and yellows. The colours were bright, bold and striking.

On this rock, he'd painted a scene around a tribal campfire with a didgeridoo player seated on a rock. The workmanship on something this size, and not a flat surface, was impressive.

Jayne handed the rock back to him. It was about the size of a closed fist, which meant not too large for people to slip into their luggage to take home. 'It's beautiful. What kind of paint do you use?'

Brendan gave a wry smile. 'They're painted in outdoor house paint, actually.'

'So it's durable.'

He nodded. 'You couldn't chip it off if you tried. And it's fade resistant.'

'Brendan, if I could offer you the right price, would you be interested in creating artworks like these for my family's tour company to offer to its tourists?'

Alex's friend was interested and they agreed to discuss it further next week.

Brendan turned to Alex then. 'There's a group of

artists I met recently. Really good work. I've organised it so you can meet them this afternoon. They're isolated. It's a four-hour drive from here.'

'Jeep hire?' Alex asked the question with the first gleam in his eyes that Jayne had seen since they'd arrived the night before. 'Bush tracks?'

'Yeah. I can't go with you. I'm climbing on to a plane myself today to go to Cairns, but the thing is—' he seemed to hesitate before he went on '—one of the elders from Alice Springs phoned me this morning. She said you'd told her you knew me. Anyway, she thought maybe you should go out there. There's one particular bloke she'd like you to meet.' He rubbed the back of his neck. 'I'd be happy to go with you—'

'But you have a plane to catch.' Alex nodded. 'No need to come along, but thanks for hand-delivering that message.'

'It could lead to another dead end in your search.'

'That's okay.' It was clear Alex had his hopes well under control.

Not so much that he wouldn't go, Jayne decided, and rushed into speech. 'We could give up the rest of today's time on tour. We thought we were going to have to lose some of it, anyway.' Jayne didn't mind. Not if it might help Alex, even if only so he could enjoy a rough-terrain drive he could pit his skills against. 'From the sounds of it, the tour programme won't be anywhere near as interesting or exciting, anyway.'

She bit her lip as she realised how that had come out.

'Well, I don't mean to say that Cutter's tours are boring. You know what I mean, Alex!'

Both men grinned and, instead of feeling embarrassed, Jayne was happy to see that smile back on Alex's face. She pushed her advantage while she had it. 'Thanks to Brendan, we already have the answer to the question of what would work ideally for the gifts for this tour. We don't need to keep looking here.'

Jayne didn't even notice she was saying 'we' all over the place.

Warmth filled Alex's eyes. 'Then I guess we're going. Thanks, Jayne, for being willing to just do that.'

'You can thank me when we've finished today's trip without me volunteering to do any of the driving,' Jayne said half teasingly, but she had to admit her limits. 'I can drive a stick shift, but I've never driven a four-wheel drive and I don't know the rules for outback dirt tracks and things.'

'I can handle the driving. I'll want area maps and I'll have to get on the phone and sort out transportation and the survival gear that needs to go with us.' Though Alex spoke the words to Brendan, he seemed to be thinking out loud.

The men put their heads together and sorted out how the trip would work and, after a strong hand grip and the request that Alex check in after his trip was done, Brendan said his goodbyes and headed away to get on with his day.

Jayne and Alex took the bus back to Alice Springs, where they would meet with a man who could hire them the right kind of vehicle and equipment. Alex wanted his arrangements in place to ensure Jayne would be safe.

That concern made Jayne half afraid, not because of Alex or the journey, but because she had a feeling there might be rather more reciprocal caring hidden inside her for this man than there should be. How could Jayne reconcile that, if indeed it was the case? Alex wasn't part of her plans for now or for the future. Not her personal plans.

Where would Jayne end up if she entered into a relationship with Alex? Would he be the first step to her downfall? Would Jayne go from a ten-year age gap to a twenty-year one, and from there to something even greater? Would she become like her father, living for each new relationship and feeling completely insecure when all of those relationships failed?

Jayne already felt insecure enough at the thought of being ten years older than a man as gorgeous as Alex. If she gave in to this interest in him, allowed her emotions to reach for him, for need for him in that way to rule her, she would be completely vulnerable. She had to protect herself from the kind of hurt that could go with those feelings.

How would she hold his affection and attention, be good enough…? She hadn't been able to do that with her own mother.

Alex had more important issues on his mind right now, anyway. Jayne wanted to support him as he worked his way through last night's meeting and through today as well. She did want that, and that was something she could give him. She told herself her thoughts couldn't be distracted in any other direction!

Alex was doing a great job of driving. Jayne drew a breath and really started to look around them. The scenery was unlike anything she had seen before. Sage-coloured spinifex dotted across flat plains. Blue sky towering overhead. Clouds banked in the distance behind them. Red dust rising in a plume behind the hired Land Rover.

'Would you like to stop for a minute, Jayne?' Alex drew the vehicle to a halt. He left the engine running and encouraged her to get out with him.

The moment she did, she experienced the stillness and the huge, uncompromising silence of the outback. She held her breath and finally turned to Alex. 'I wouldn't want to get lost out here.'

Yet somehow the sense of space made her feel rather lost, anyway. Lost, and awed by this creation, and conscious that…Alex had been lost and someone, somewhere out here held the key for him to understand his past.

Brendan had wanted Alex to make this trip…

Jayne wanted it to bring answers for Alex. There were no answers for her—only the knowledge that it could do nothing but hurt, to trace a woman who wanted nothing of her daughters, her granddaughter, or the life she had lived before leaving Jayne's father.

'Thanks for stopping, Alex.' Jayne let herself absorb

their surroundings; let the peace push away those un-happy thoughts.

She wasn't sure why they were so strong at the mo-ment. Because Jayne was at a crossroads in her working life—a make or break point that could separate her from the work she did for and with her father?

When they got back into the Land Rover, they trav-elled in silence for a few minutes. Jayne let her gaze shift to the window. A wind had started to blow and the sky looked turbulent in the distance, dusty and brooding rather than just those few clouds that had been hover-ing. Jayne suppressed a sigh. She felt conflicted inside, between her business instincts and other instincts, be-tween wanting Alex and feeling it was not safe to let that interest develop.

Alex had asked earlier if she minded that he was the middleman with any art arrangements with Brendan. Jayne wouldn't dream of trying to cut Alex out of that; her business professionalism demanded it. But, when Alex had asked, the first thought in Jayne's mind had been that they were partners, in this together. And that feeling felt far too right and covered too much ground within Jayne's thoughts—ground that wasn't only about work.

She missed Alex's touch—his mouth on hers, his arms around her. They'd only kissed once and Jayne had told him that must not happen again and yet, without ad-mitting it to herself, she had wished for it every moment since, whether she'd allowed herself to acknowledge that fact or not. And Alex had agreed it mustn't happen again.

'I think that's it ahead.' Alex gestured with a fingertip lifted from the steering wheel. A small cluster of buildings materialised out of the seemingly endless dirt track.

They pulled to a stop on the outskirts of the settlement. Jayne glanced out of the window at two small children who'd come to see what the visitors were about. Dusky faces, curly black hair and the biggest, deepest, brownest eyes Jayne had seen stared up at her.

Jayne opened the door and got out, and Alex followed suit. She smiled at the children. 'Hello.'

Shy grins came her way before the two darted off again. Jayne breathed the hot air into her lungs and shook her head. 'How can they run like that in this weather?'

'Kids can be pretty tough.' Alex glanced about them. 'Let's go find our artists. That building over there looks promising.' His shoulders were set like concrete. 'I guess the rest will unfold. Brendan didn't give me a name, but he said he'd phone to say I was on my way.'

Jayne moved to his side, ready to do whatever she could to be supportive. 'I hope this all works out for you, Alex. That it's a worthwhile trip.'

Oh, yes. Jayne was controlling her care factor towards Alex totally, right along with the attraction factor and the interest factor!

CHAPTER EIGHT

'THANK you for the privilege of seeing you all painting.' Jayne spoke the words about an hour later as she and Alex stood inside the building he had pointed out. It was a shed with a concrete floor and corrugated iron sides and roof—large, with one whole end opened up for air and light and heaps of room inside for the artists to paint.

The artists were men and women of various ages. Some preferred to sit on the floor to paint directly onto the pieces of linen or canvas. Others sat at tables. The artworks included depictions of desert sand, storms brewing, leaves and grasses, flowers and seedpods.

Alex asked if he could look through a pile of completed canvases resting on several trestle tables in one corner of the shed.

He'd been very controlled through this visit. Polite, friendly and businesslike as he dealt with the initial shyness of some of the artists. Too controlled. He must have had questions, must want to know which person out here might have answers for him. Brendan had paved the way for the visit. When would that person be revealed?

Jayne wouldn't have been able to wait. She'd have wanted to ask all these questions outright. But it was a small settlement, and the people here had their ways with things. Jayne just hoped Alex wasn't burning up inside too much from the need to know.

It was as Alex moved to the trestle tables that one of the older men, who'd worked silently at his artwork throughout the visit, rose and walked over.

'I spoke with Brendan Carroll about your visit. He said you were looking for your family history out here.'

These were the words Jayne had waited for and, when she glanced at Alex, she caught the sudden, quickly masked tension that for a moment filled his expression.

Jayne stopped where she was, a few feet away from them. The other artists seemed content to continue working and Jayne returned to join them.

Though she gave her attention to the work going on in front of her, she could still hear Alex's response to the man.

'That's right. I spoke with some elders in Alice Springs last night but I got nowhere.' Alex looked directly into the man's face. 'You know my name. The surname is one I chose a few years ago. I was left at an orphanage with the names "Alex Roy" pinned to my clothing. No last name, so they called me Alex Roy "Jordan" after a nearby street. Later on, I changed the last name to MacKay. I'm looking for answers about aspects of my parentage.'

He drew a deep breath and blew it out. 'Sorry. I guess the need to know goes deeper than I'd realised. I'm a bit tense right now.'

The older man searched Alex's face. 'Will you tell me what's your age? Your birth date?'

'I don't know the exact birth date. I got given one at the orphanage where I grew up.' Alex told him that date and year.

With a remote part of her mind, Jayne registered that she had correctly guessed his age. But, in this moment, that disparity was far less of concern than the conversation going on between the two men.

'What else do you know about your history?'

Why was the older man asking questions, instead of trying to answer Alex's for him? And what was his name?

'My mother grew up in Alice Springs, left me anonymously on the doorstep of a Sydney orphanage when I was a baby, and only revealed anything about herself to me in a letter that I received a few weeks ago after her…after her death.' Alex drew another breath. 'She was Lizzie Perry.'

Jayne's heart squeezed as she registered Alex's words. He said it all as though it were nothing but matter-of-fact, but it was that history that was responsible for his maturity, for who he was. Knowing all of this, Jayne admired him twice as much for his good-humoured outlook on life, for the cheeky streak in his otherwise mature and steady nature that made him complex and at the same time so very appealing as a man.

She wanted to go to Alex, tuck her arm through his, but she had to wait here and let this play out, give him the space to do this by himself.

The older man's hand rose to clasp his shoulder. 'When Brendan phoned, I didn't want to get my hopes up until I'd met you for myself. I've been watching you since you got here. My heart knew, but I had to ask the questions, too.'

Jayne's surroundings faded from her consciousness as she held her breath. Was this Alex's answer?

Alex's face paled beneath the tanned skin and tension locked his expression into one of waiting, of hope held back. Of needing to know and perhaps not wanting to admit how much he needed that knowledge.

'I'm not sure what it is that you know.' Alex's voice was deep and so, so guarded. He said gruffly, 'Are you saying you think you know something about my past?'

'Yeah. I know.' The older man's smile was a mixture of gentleness and regret and acceptance. He, too, seemed shaken.

And there was something in that gentleness that Jayne had seen before—had seen in Alex. She took a step towards them before she realised it, and abruptly stopped again.

'You *were* given your last name. It's the same as my half-brother's name. We had different fathers.' The man drew a breath and the creases in his face seemed to deepen. 'He was Peter Roy. He passed away eleven years ago. I'm Morgan Garrup. I'm your uncle.' His eyes glistened with moisture. 'I always prayed you'd find your way to your history. I wasn't sure if I'd ever meet you, but I am very glad.'

'Are you sure of what you're saying?' Alex swallowed once, and again. 'My birth was never registered. I had nothing to go on.'

'Except a need to find your roots here, I'm guessing.' Morgan watched Alex carefully. 'When you come from out here, especially when there's blood inside you that's been here for so long, there's a part of you that needs to know.'

'That's how I've felt.' Alex ran a hand over the back of his head. The vulnerable gesture made Jayne want, more than ever, to go to him.

'I'm sure of who you are, Alex. I met your mother. It was only once, but she was already in the early stages of pregnancy with you at that time.' The rest of Morgan's story wasn't great, but it did confirm that he had no doubts about Alex's identity.

The older man was shamed to say his brother hadn't wanted a baby. By the time Morgan had caught up with his brother again to ask about the baby, the relationship between Alex's parents had ended. The woman had been long gone. Morgan had assumed she must have kept Alex with her but he'd had no idea how to find either of them. Or even Alex's name or gender. 'You look very much like your late father, too. I'd like to know you, Alex. If you want, I can tell you about your history. Who you are. All of that.'

'I'd like that.' Alex turned then, sought Jayne's

gaze. The invitation was in his eyes and Jayne hurried to his side.

Alex couldn't quite get the shocked and stunned expression off his face, but he introduced Jayne, put into words what he'd just been told. 'This is my uncle, Morgan Garrup, Jayne.' His tone deepened. 'I have an uncle.'

That one vulnerable statement brought moisture to the backs of Jayne's eyes. She blinked and pasted the biggest, widest smile on her face that she could manage as she shook the older man's hand. 'I'm so pleased to meet you, Mr Garrup.'

Jayne chatted on with the older man for a couple of minutes. In that time, she sensed Alex trying to pull himself together at her side. She felt privileged to be part of this, and particularly while his emotions were exposed in this way. Jayne wanted to hold him close, let him express whatever feelings this had brought to the surface for him.

They spoke for a while longer until one of the other settlement residents came in to speak a few brief words. 'News just came over the radio that there's a bad dust storm on the way. It's going to stop movement in the area, by the sounds of it.'

'You should leave, nephew.' Morgan spoke the words quietly.

Resistance came immediately to Alex's face before he glanced at Jayne and his expression became even more torn.

'We can stay—' Jayne began.

'I don't want to leave you yet…Uncle Morgan.' Alex seemed to have to work to bring the words out.

Morgan clasped Alex's shoulder then. 'We have time. You'll come back when you can visit for a few days. You need to come to terms with finding me. I…need that time, too.'

'Alex, can I go and start getting paintings packed ready for transit while you finish up here?' Jayne thought that might be best—give Alex what time she could with his uncle.

Alex nodded a little numbly before he seemed to clear his thoughts a little. 'Thanks. Speak to Sue. She knows what I'm going to take.'

Morgan and Alex both turned to speak further with the man who'd brought the weather report, while Jayne went to organise the artworks with Sue.

When Alex joined Jayne outside at their vehicle, he looked pale but was obviously making an effort to be composed. 'We need to go, Jayne.'

His uncle had come out with him. Alex turned to the older man now. 'I have the phone number for your niece so I can get in contact with you. You have my number.'

Morgan patted his shirt pocket, where a piece of paper crackled. 'Right here.'

'Right.' Alex swallowed. 'I'll be back soon. Within a couple of weeks. You won't have gone—'

'I'll be here.' Morgan's eyes, which must have seen so much over the years, softened. He clasped Alex's forearm and used the grip to pull him into a one-armed hug.

Jayne fought back her emotion as Alex clasped the other man's shoulder and, for a brief moment, bent his head. Grey hair to dark hair, the two men showed their biological similarities in the curve of the sides of their faces, the shape of the backs of their heads.

Alex drew away.

Morgan glanced at the sky, and then at Alex. 'You must be careful to go the way I said.' His eyes glistened before he turned away.

Alex got in the Land Rover and they drove away.

Jayne drew a slow breath. 'I've heard that some Aboriginal people don't like to say goodbye as they feel it can be bad luck.' She hesitated. 'I'm so glad you met him, Alex.'

'Yeah.' Alex's throat worked as he swallowed. 'I can hardly take it in. I…didn't expect to feel so overwhelmed by finding someone…related.'

He'd found more than that. He'd found open arms. A welcome from a family member, instead of the rejection he'd received at the hands of his mother and, whether he ever experienced it first-hand or not, also from his father.

'Are you quite sure you don't want to stay, Alex?' That was the most urgent question on Jayne's mind right now. And she would give up being back in Sydney by Friday, if need be, to give Alex that time with his uncle.

'I appreciate the offer, Jayne, but I think Morgan was

right. I do need time to get my head around this and, for now, to drive us to safety so we can get out of here. I need…to take this news to my brothers face to face, too.' He gestured behind them as he turned, not in the direction they'd taken to get here, but along a track to the left. 'Morgan needs the time, too.'

'We're not going back the way we came?' Jayne glanced behind them. A ball of rolling dust seemed to be growing in the distance.

'No. We're driving north-west for about another hour.' Alex's hands tightened on the wheel as he navigated a particularly bumpy stretch of road. 'We can't go back.'

'Where are we going now?' Jayne didn't question Alex making the decision about that 'where' without consulting her. She trusted him.

More than you can trust your father with his decisions that impact on you.

Yet Jayne *had* trusted her father. She'd trusted him with her working career.

And where did that get you, Jayne?

That was her battle. Her father had let her work up to a good job at Cutter's. But he'd also made a promise that he hadn't kept since Eric came along, and Jayne felt that hadn't been fair. She'd worked hard and even without the proposal she was putting together now to put to her father, she had more than earned her partnership.

So no. Perhaps she didn't trust her father in some ways. He'd let her down with that, and he'd let her mother go…

Oh, Jayne. You can't blame him for that. You don't know why she made that decision.

Why did Jayne trust Alex the way she did? In the middle of the outback, headed away from where they'd come from to…Jayne had no idea where, when she'd known Alex a bare few days?

But she did, and maybe that was because she'd seen his calibre as a man in circumstances that might have been rather hard on him, especially in the past twenty-four hours. And maybe it was just because somehow she knew she could.

'We can get flown out of here. Before we left the settlement my uncle…Morgan asked one of the others to make the arrangements for us.' Alex navigated a deeply corrugated stretch of track and increased his speed again once they got past it. 'There's a bush pilot. He does deliveries, mail runs and a few other things. He's prepared to fly us in a round trip avoiding the storm, back to Alice Springs.'

'How bad is it going to be back at the settlement? Will the people we met all be safe?'

'They'll be okay. Morgan says they've dealt with this sort of thing plenty of times before.'

That was something, at least. But Alex's tone…Oh, Jayne desperately wanted to wrap her arms around him, but that wasn't possible right now.

'I need to concentrate on driving now, Jayne. I don't want to lose a minute of time to outrun this.' Alex's hands tightened on the steering wheel as he again navigated a particularly hazardous stretch of road.

He was pitting his skill against the conditions. This wasn't thrill-seeking. It was a combination of knowing himself, being confident in what he knew he could do, measuring conditions and strength. He had things on his mind right now, huge things, but even in the face of those he was making sure he and Jayne were safe. He showed a lot of courage and control.

Jayne could learn a lot from Alex MacKay.

'Hold tight.' As Alex spoke the words, Jayne gasped as he steered around a large rock that had seemed to appear in the middle of the track from nowhere.

A moment later, they were moving normally again.

The road opened out and Alex released a slow breath before his hands relaxed a little on the wheel. 'We should only be about half an hour from the pilot's home now. He lives by himself and there's no one around in any direction for quite a stretch.'

'It would be a very different life out here.' Jayne was beginning to really understand that. She choked a little. 'Sorry. The dust—'

'As well as what's coming up off the track as we drive, the storm is catching up with us faster than I'd like.' As Alex spoke, he glanced in the rear-view mirror and frowned.

Jayne looked over her shoulder and was very glad they weren't too far from shelter now because that ball of red dust seemed to have expanded behind them, covering everything in its approach.

'We'll beat it,' Alex said with determination. 'We're not getting stuck in that.'

Finally, they came to the end of their journey—to the sight of a hangar with a home built into one end of it, and to…

'The plane's leaving!' Jayne stared at the view of the aircraft as it lifted off the end of the runway into the sky. 'He's leaving without us!'

The pilot had indeed left and, when they stopped their vehicle outside the building and got out, there was a note taped sturdily to the door:

Sorry, folks. There's been an accident. Make yourselves at home and, whatever you do, stay indoors until the radio broadcasts confirm that this storm is over. I'll be back to fly you out as soon as I can manage it.

'At least there's decent shelter.' Alex turned the door handle. When the door swung open he gestured for Jayne to go in. 'I'll get the Land Rover under cover. Back in a minute.'

'Okay.' Jayne went inside. It wasn't a large home, just a few rooms built into the end of the hangar, but the pilot had made the space his own. Jayne heard the scrape of large metal doors, an engine starting. By the time she'd looked at the living room, the shelves full of vinyl records, a coffee cup on the bench in the small kitchen and a percolator still warm and sending its aroma all through the cosy space, Alex had stepped inside and closed the door behind him.

He had the large cooler from the Land Rover in one

hand and Jayne's handbag in the other. He set her bag down inside the door and placed the cooler on the floor in the kitchen.

Jayne went to him then. She didn't want to push, but he seemed to understand instinctively and he let her in. The hug they shared was long and silent, a giving and taking that Jayne couldn't explain. Finally, Alex drew back and looked down into her eyes with very deep, very blue eyes.

'Thanks,' he said almost gruffly, and turned back to the cooler and removed two bottles from it. 'I'm sorry we're stuck here, Jayne. This wasn't quite how I planned for this trip to end today.'

'There's no apology needed. You're not responsible for the weather. I'm just sorry we're here when we could have stayed with your uncle. But you got answers today. That's really good, Alex.'

Let me…

Jayne didn't even know what she was silently asking, except that she needed to give him whatever he needed, if she even could. 'It's all right. We'll leave when we can.' She took several deep swallows of the water. 'Thank you. I needed that. Alex—'

'Same here. It's been quite a day.' His gaze examined hers and he gestured to the sofa. 'Feel like sitting a while? I've got so many thoughts going around in my head, I don't think I'm going to be good for much else for a while until I get them sorted out.'

They sat side by side. Little pinging sounds started to hit the outside walls and the windows of the pilot's home. Alex glanced towards those closed windows before he turned back to her. 'We're safe here while the storm rolls through. Provided we stay inside and keep things closed up, the worst will be some dust getting inside.'

The pilot's home closed up well and Jayne doubted there'd be too much dust invasion. 'I'm not worried.'

'It will be worse back at the settlement.' Alex shook his head. 'I admit I'm not sorry to have left. I needed time to absorb what I was told today. I have my answers now.' He shook his head. 'I'm surprised. I thought I'd hit a wall and that I'd never know, but one of the elders I saw last night got thinking and dredged up a memory.'

'How did Brendan come into it?' Jayne had wondered about that.

'He knew the elder. I mentioned that I knew Brendan and that I was hoping to see him today if he could free up any time.'

'So the elder phoned Brendan?'

'Yes, because Brendan knew Morgan out at the settlement.'

And that was why Brendan had wished he could have gone with Alex.

'Morgan seemed as though he really wanted to know you.' It made Jayne angry that Alex's father had not. Angry for Alex and…angry for herself as well because parents shouldn't do that. They shouldn't just walk away or turn their back before they ever knew a child, either. For Alex, both parents had done it. 'You'll come back out soon—let Morgan give you some history about this part of yourself? Does it help, Alex? Does this help fill the void of not knowing?'

'It…does.' As he said it he seemed to come to accept the fact. 'Yes. It does help. I needed to know where I'd come from. I got the added bonus of an uncle who wants to know me. I need to share this with my brothers. I'm not sure how I feel about that just yet, but I do have my answers now.'

Jayne had her answers, too, really. Her mother had left without explanation or a backward glance. That might feel unpalatable and…it always had. But that was what Jayne had.

'You helped, Jayne. Without this trip, who knows when I might have got out here or whether those particular puzzle pieces would have fallen into place.' He hesitated. 'I wish I could give *you* more than the knowledge…'

'That my mother left? It was a long time ago.' She wanted to say the platitude that it was okay; it didn't even bother her any more. But it did bother Jayne. Mostly, she tried not to think about it but she knew she would always feel abandoned. Angry. Confused. Alex's situation had been the same, and he wouldn't suddenly stop having those feelings about it. But he had a chance to know a relative who wanted to know him. That was nice.

'Sometimes there are things in life that aren't right.'

'That's certainly true.' Jayne drew a breath and a smile pushed through her emotion and spread until she couldn't hold it back. 'I am so happy for you, Alex.

You've gained a relative you didn't know you had, and a greater sense of your history and who you are.'

'I have, haven't I?' He smiled, too, and blew out a breath.

Time had passed as they spoke, and Jayne got up. She sensed Alex could do with dropping the topic for now. 'Are you hungry? Let's see if we can find something to eat.'

She knew the pilot wouldn't mind. He'd made it clear they were welcome here until he got back.

Alex joined her and they rummaged through the cupboards and refrigerator. They found tinned soup, and bread in the freezer, and a shake-and-make pancake mix that just needed water to be added.

Alex lined it all up on the kitchen bench and raised his brows, and Jayne laughed and shrugged. 'Why not? We don't care if it's a bit of a weird combination, do we?'

They'd talked about some intense things today. Alex had experienced some intense things. It did feel good now, to relax in the small kitchen area to put together a simple meal and sit at the dining table to eat.

Jayne looked across that small table towards the end of the meal and she thought of just how much her emotions had become involved in Alex today. She'd made that connection with him in a different way as the story of his past had unfolded. Jayne felt so privileged to have been there for that—privileged and very soft inside for Alex with all of this. How had she let her emotions become so wrapped up in Alex when she'd promised herself she wouldn't let that happen?

Because it had and, whether she wanted to blame it all on the personal ground Alex had covered last night and today in relation to family, Jayne knew it was a lot more really even than all that. She'd bonded somehow with Alex as she'd never connected to any other man.

This fact—inexplicable, challenging and scary—was something Jayne didn't know how to manage or control or keep within any boundaries she might set.

'Are you all right, Jayne?' Alex leaned across the table to briefly touch her hand. 'We've talked about me, but what about you? If today has raised bad memories for you I'm going to be very sorry.'

'No. Don't think that.' Jayne's gaze locked with his. 'I admit it is painful thinking back to the loss of my mother but not because of you, Alex. I can't get the kind of responses you got today about my past. There's no one out there waiting to connect. Mum knows where Cutter's is. She could make contact through the office at any time if she chose. So I'm just reconciled that her choice to leave, for whatever reasons, won't ever turn around. An explanation would have been nice, but I don't expect to ever have that, either.'

'I guess for both of us there's good and bad in our family histories.' He didn't refer directly to his father not wanting to know of his existence. Jayne understood, anyway.

Alex changed the subject then. 'Have you thought

more about the offer from the Lis? Would you consider working for them?'

'I'd like to know more about their offer.' Jayne wasn't sure where she would go from there. But she was interested.

Alex nodded. 'Then let's see if there's phone reception here. I think we both need to make some calls.'

CHAPTER NINE

WHILE Jayne spoke on her mobile with Mr Li, Alex
called Brendan and filled him in on the outcome of
his trip. He then contacted Morgan's relative and asked
the woman to pass on the message that Alex was safe
and sound. After that, he phoned the hotel in Alice
Springs. He asked them to pack and store his and Jayne's
luggage ready for collection and explained what had
happened.

Jayne was thoughtful after her call to the Lis, but
silent on that topic. Alex chose not to push for information and hoped she would tell him of her own accord
eventually.

The day and evening passed, and the dust storm
played out while they sat side by side talking on the
sofa. Jayne took a break to work on her proposal to her
father. The pilot's radio set came to life several times
with reports about the storm and the progress of their
missing pilot.

'The radio is interesting listening, I'll give it that,'
Alex said as another burst of chat subsided. 'It seems

a great way for people around the region to keep in contact.'

By listening to the broadcasts, Jayne and Alex had learned that the pilot had landed safely with his injured cargo, who was now receiving the much-needed medical treatment. The flying doctor service for the area had already been busy elsewhere, and that trip was also looking as though it would have a positive outcome.

The outcome of the dust storm wouldn't be known until tomorrow morning. That piece of feedback had frustrated Jayne. She'd stared at the radio as though willing it to offer more information.

Alex had teasingly said she could get on there and ask, but his intrepid Jayne had quickly shaken her head. 'I don't know the protocols for using it.' Jayne had spoken the words in a prissy version of her beautiful smooth voice.

She'd still sounded sexy as hell. Alex had been fighting the ever growing awareness of her since they'd arrived here. He'd driven with a storm brewing behind them, had felt the need to protect her, get her to safety.

In the middle of all that he'd been coming to terms with meeting his uncle, with finding answers to questions that had been with him throughout his lifetime.

Jayne had so clearly wanted to be happy for him and comfort him if he needed that. The soft, womanly response was not only generous because of her history. It had made Alex feel good, had only made him want Jayne more.

He wanted Jayne back in his arms again. It was that

complicated, and that simple. The tensions of a few days, the questions of a lifetime. Affinity with a woman whose mother had abandoned the family. Affinity with Jayne, because she was Jayne.

They took showers and then talked about Jayne's family—her niece, her sister who was younger than Jayne. About Alex's brothers, the landscaping business Brent and Fiona ran together, and Linc's chain of plant nurseries.

It helped Alex to talk about Linc and Brent—helped to get all of his thoughts about family back into perspective. 'What I really want to do is to take my brothers to meet Morgan. I won't tell them about this until I get back to Sydney. I'd rather do it face to face, but yeah, that's what I'd like to do.'

'You're all very successful,' Jayne said. 'You most of all, Alex, because you've got where you are so early in your working career.'

'The need to provide safety and security for us drove Brent and Linc to try to make money.' Alex remembered Brent's determination, how hard his brother had worked because it was the one thing he could do until he got Linc, and then Alex out of the orphanage.

At the time, though those sacrifices had meant the world to him, Alex's restlessness had been at its peak. 'I didn't always make things easy for them while I was still in that orphanage.'

Jayne's face creased into a smile that was a combination of understanding and wryness. 'Did you get into a lot of trouble, Alex?'

She let her gaze drop to his hands and reached out with her fingertips to touch two small scars on the back of one of them. 'I wondered how you got these. I thought there might have been a bit of a story behind them.'

'Most people don't even notice them.' Yet he wasn't really surprised that Jayne had.

Alex's fingers meshed with hers. Maybe he shouldn't have taken that touch, but he did, and it felt right to thread his fingers through hers, to look at the contrast of his strong fingers with Jayne's soft, ladylike ones. 'I got the scars running away one night after I'd…expressed my opinion about a few core issues in an inappropriate form and place. I discovered I had a handy knack with a can of spray paint.'

He'd needed to do something to let his energy out. What he'd really needed was to get out of the orphanage and be with his brothers. The wait for that had come at a time in his teenage years when he hadn't been able to manage himself as well as he otherwise might have. 'I was a bit reckless for a while. I regret that, but I did grow out of it.'

'And turned to abseiling and other sports and activities to satisfy your need for a challenge and excitement.' Jayne's fingers felt warm in his.

Her words were warm too, and understanding. They accepted, rather than judged. And they teased, just a little, as she went on, 'You're still getting all of the fun with your adrenalin sports, but without getting into trouble over it. I'm guessing your brothers are relieved about that.'

'Yeah, actually they are.' His grin held good humour before it faded and he went on, 'I turned to business, as well. Maybe that's what all of us did when we got free of that place—set out to make money because at least then we'd be sure we had a roof over our heads, food on the table and nobody would be able to separate us from each other.'

'I admire you…' Jayne's words trailed off as her gaze locked with his.

'That's mutual, you know.' As was the tide of desire that flowed between them. It didn't seem to ever leave. Today it had been there, simmering beneath the surface, waiting for its time and place.

Was there any control at all for either of them with that? Alex had never felt so out of control in his response to a woman. His other hand wanted to cup the back of her neck, bring her closer. 'You've faced your own set of challenges. A fractured family, raising your sister.'

'My father withholding a partnership from me after he said I was due for it, all because of a new employee he favours more.' Jayne hadn't meant to say the words, but here, in this setting with her…heart so open to Alex, they slipped out.

Open because Alex had been through a lot emotionally today.

Jayne hastened to put her reactions into that perspective.

Alex frowned. 'Your father has stopped you reaching the peak of your working career in the family company?'

'That doesn't impact on the proposal we're working on together—'

'I'm not worried about that,' he said without hesitation. 'I know I can trust your word. I'm just concerned that your talent and achievements aren't being acknowledged.'

Jayne drew a breath. 'I didn't mean to criticise my father in front of you. I…let my guard down with you.'

That was a gift to Alex, even if it did make Jayne feel uncomfortable to have exposed her workplace vulnerabilities.

'Thank you for giving me that gift, Jayne. I won't say anything, but I'd like to help you if there's some way that I can.'

'There is, actually.' This was something Jayne had been thinking about since she'd first spoken with him at their Monday meeting. 'I'd like you to come with me when I present my proposal to my father. If I can ask you to speak in person about your company, the gifts you'll be supplying, I think that can only strengthen the impact of the overall proposal.'

'I'll be happy to.' He just made his commitment to it, there and then.

Jayne nodded. 'I'll let my father know you'll be there with me.'

'In the meantime—' Alex hesitated, then seemed to make a decision and went on '—what happens with your promotion?'

'I've spoken to my father and explained how I feel

about him holding back on the promotion.' Jayne didn't go into more detail—it wasn't necessary. Instead, she just went on, 'I've been thinking about it and I'm going to take the offer from the Lis to do the voicing for their virtual tours.'

Jayne blew out a breath because it felt a little scary, but also good to make the commitment. 'While you were in the shower earlier I phoned Mr Li a second time and we made our agreement. I start work on the voice recordings a month from now. I see that as a bargaining chip to use with my father, an indication to him that I can and will take work elsewhere if I feel I can't progress any further in the family company, though the work with the Lis will only be part-time.'

'Congratulations on making that choice, Jayne.' Pleasure for her shone in his eyes.

'I would have told you sooner—' she gave a wry laugh '—but I was busy feeling a little freaked out about it.' She hadn't minded taking time to convince herself she hadn't just done something way too radical and possibly risky. 'I don't regret it. It'll mean dropping three days a fortnight from my job at Cutter's, to make time to do the recordings for the Lis. It'll be a two-year contract and, to be honest, it's going to be quite lucrative. I do truly hope that taking that on will make Dad sit up and take notice.'

'I hope so.' Alex's words were soft. Gentle.

Deep.

Jayne didn't know when she'd got to her feet but Alex was there beside her. And, when she lifted her face and let her gaze meet his, the blue of his eyes was deep and there was tightness across his cheekbones that told her that he desired her and, in this moment, he needed her.

Jayne had fought that feeling and now she lost the fight. When Alex lowered his mouth towards hers, Jayne raised her lips to his and…kissed him.

Jayne took this second kiss with Alex with her senses and her desire and her attraction and the closeness they had built through the revelation of family circumstances. And with feelings that were deep inside her. Still unnamed, but there.

'Jayne,' he whispered, 'I want you so much.'

If she gave in to this, they would make love here in the desert in a pilot's hangar, surrounded by vast silence and red dust and everything that was at the core of nature in this stunning heart of their country.

So many things passed through Jayne's mind—so much insecurity about age, appeal, being someone who could engender strong abiding feelings in anyone.

Need for Alex pushed those fears back into their dark place.

In Alex's steady blue gaze Jayne only saw encouragement and a chance to give to him all that she felt, all of her desire. She wasn't a cougar. She was just…a woman.

If Alex wanted her, wanted this, then Jayne would take what they could share. And then they would find their way back to Sydney one way or another and this would be over.

It couldn't be any other way, could it? A tight feeling

rose in Jayne's chest and squeezed, and she pushed it away. 'I want this, too, Alex.'

He searched her face. 'I don't have protection.'

'I'm on the Pill.'

'Thank you…for this,' he whispered and reached out his arms to her. And he kissed her gently—so gently, letting his lips brush over hers, savouring each moment of connection with her.

Jayne found something inside herself when Alex kissed her like that—something that opened her emotions and let him in, even to parts of her that she didn't understand.

Jayne's arms rose. She felt the sturdy muscles in the sides of his neck and knew his strength and wanted to give herself to all of his strength and so she did.

But Alex gave, too. His hand rose to stroke the side of her face from her jaw to her temple and he sighed into her mouth as he kissed her, and Jayne felt as though she'd given him a gift, that she had given him something that he had needed very much.

Just as he had given to her, too. Warning bells were there, but he took her hand and led her to the neat second bedroom with its plain double bed and sparse furnishings.

'Are we out of our depth, Jayne?' he asked and in the backs of his eyes the question lingered. Desire for her and so many other emotions lingered. It didn't matter if she couldn't name them.

They were all within her, also, each feeling of hers answering all that her senses and emotions found in him—vulnerability, too. Was she wrong to think that was in both of them? Why would Alex—? 'I don't know, Alex. All I know is that this feels right for now, for tonight.' If she didn't ask for too much, then she wasn't committing too much of herself.

'This moment.' Something in his expression stilled, but then he blinked and whatever it was, was gone. He wrapped his arms around her, all the way around so that they were body to body, heartbeat to heartbeat, and he kissed her again.

Jayne felt filled with need in a way she had never felt before. She felt these things for Alex, with Alex.

Her fingers gripped the hem of his T-shirt and she pushed it up. He reached behind his neck and pulled the T-shirt over his head and threw it onto the floor. His body was beautiful, perfect, and Jayne's balance tipped from one instant to the next as a surge of fear and inadequacy rose. She hesitated.

'Let me see you, Jayne. Please—' his deep voice filled with longing '—I've wanted so much...'

Jayne let down her guard somewhere in the depth of his gaze. Her shirt followed his and she did think about her softness, the parts of her body that weren't lean and fit, that matched her age and didn't match his age.

She had never felt like this. Was that why uncertainty also rose? Or was it because of his perfection? He wasn't a Drew or a George or any of the older men Jayne had dated. This was a different playing field and Jayne wasn't totally sure she was safe and secure to play.

Alex's hands rose to stroke over the indent of her waist, up her sides, and he whispered, 'You're so beautiful, Jayne.'

So being older didn't matter. It didn't, did it?

The rest of their clothes fell away, a scatter across the floor as Alex learned each part of her, and Jayne learned each part of him.

Jayne lay with her head on the pillow and looked into Alex's gaze above her. She didn't remember how they'd got there, but they had and they'd spent aeons in each other's arms, and moments that weren't enough, that demanded that they hold each other tighter, linger longer, draw even closer.

They were on the brink of a journey, but the journey had somehow started from the moment they'd met. 'Make love to me, Alex, because I want…and need to make love to you.'

'Jayne…' Alex had no words, only his touch and his embrace as he invested all of himself in this moment with Jayne.

She hadn't wanted him to see her body. She had hesitated, yet she was so beautiful. How did he show her that? How did he do that and understand the feelings tightening his chest right now, making him feel protective of Jayne and desperate for her, all at once?

Until now, Alex had separated intimacy and emotion. With Jayne, he had blurred that line, disintegrated it. So much emotion in such a short span of time. Getting his answers…and this. Because it was emotion, even if he didn't understand all of that.

'Alex,' she whispered against his neck as he kissed her over and over.

Alex held Jayne against his heart. He offered his body and his emotions were in that offering, even if he didn't want to fully confront that fact.

He held Jayne and he gave to her and she gave to him and in that moment, when everything was stripped away for both of them, Alex thought that he didn't ever want to let Jayne go.

How did he feel so deeply for a woman—for Jayne—when he didn't know how to do that, or what that meant?

Alex brushed damp tendrils of wavy hair from Jayne's forehead and his fingers brushed over the fine lines that fanned out at the sides of her eyes and crinkled so endearingly when she smiled. He wanted to speak, but still the words wouldn't come. Alex didn't have answers to all of this.

Jayne felt Alex's fingers touch the wrinkles at the sides of her eyes. She was overwhelmed by what they had shared, shattered inside from the sense of having yielded herself so deeply to him. Her emotions were vulnerable, every weakness and fear too willing to surface.

She wanted to turn her head away and not let him touch those parts of her that underlined that she was older—that Alex was more physically appealing and, no matter how much time might pass, that fact would never change because the age gap would always be there.

She'd had silly thoughts about a flirty, older woman/

younger man scenario but in those imaginary situations the woman was powerful and confident and the man more than willing to be with her. Attracted to her, attractive to her.

Jayne's need for Alex had pushed past her uncertainties, but now the balance seemed to tip the other way.

Jayne didn't turn her head away. Instead, she pressed into Alex's touch, met his gaze and hoped all he saw was happiness and completion in her eyes because she did feel those things, and they were what she most wanted to feel right now. Jayne couldn't face the negative emotions.

She swallowed hard and brushed her fingers softly over the side of his jaw and across his neck. They made love again, then, and Jayne let all her thoughts slide away on waves of sensation in Alex's arms.

Later, they drifted on the edge of slumber. 'Sleep, Jayne.' Alex brushed the lightest of kisses over her brow and turned her in his arms so they could sleep spooned with her back against his chest. Maybe he had no idea and, if that was the case, then that was probably best because they'd committed to tonight and that was all, and Jayne would rather he didn't know any of her fears.

If she slept, then perhaps in the morning Jayne would find the strength to go forward from here without the sense of loss that she had a feeling might come. Jayne closed her eyes…

She woke confused and disoriented in a strange bed. There were voices outside somewhere and—

'Alex.' Remembrance washed over her and she came fully awake in a startled, comprehending rush that cut through all her defences before she could stop it.

She'd fallen in love with Alex. That was why last night had meant so much, why her feelings had cut so deep. The pleasure and joy of making love with him, and the corresponding fear and uncertainty afterwards.

Why did you let this happen, Jayne?

Why had she let herself fall in love with him when he'd said he only wanted that night together? She'd set herself up for a fall when she should have known better because Jayne had never managed to hold the love of anyone who mattered, except for Nickie, and her sister had only had Jayne out of a less than stellar bunch of choices, anyway.

'I can't do this.' Panic flooded through Jayne because if she let these feelings rise to the surface she would have to deal with them, and how could she do that when even the thought of having such intense need for Alex terrified her?

Because she was older, and she wasn't in the prime of her twenties as he was...

And Alex. What were Alex's feelings after last night? He hadn't expected this to turn into a love affair. He'd made it clear that it was about the moment. So, Alex wasn't in love with Jayne. That was clear.

Jayne nodded and a little heavy lump settled somewhere in the centre of her chest. But she'd faced tough things before. She could face this down, too. She'd just tell Alex.

What? The question resonated inside Jayne and she swung her feet over the edge of the bed and sat up.

They had to work together. How could she do that and not think about what had happened?

You've done the same thing your father did, Jayne. You've committed emotionally to someone younger who can't give you what you need from him.

Jayne had fallen in love with Alex, but Alex hadn't fallen in love with Jayne.

'It's good that you were able to fly back in.' Alex's words sounded somewhere not too far away outside the bedroom window.

He was clearly speaking to the pilot, and Jayne couldn't even hear his voice without aching inside.

Alex went on, 'And thank you for making your home available to us while you were gone. We appreciated that.'

His voice was morning deep, a little rough. Was he thinking of Jayne—wishing he still had her in his arms? Or wishing he'd never taken last night's step at all?

A man's voice responded. 'That's the way of things out here. Couldn't have you both roaming around in a dust storm. It'll be easy enough to fly you back to Alice Springs this morning. There's a flight you'll be able to catch from there.'

So that was done. Dust storm over. They could get their hire vehicle collected from out here, fly back to Alice Springs and then to Sydney. Jayne would put her proposal to her father and she believed he would approve it. Then she'd tell him she wanted her partnership. If he gave it to her, everything would be fine. If not, she would leave Cutter's. And Alex would go his way.

Jayne gathered up her clothes and hurried towards the bathroom. She hadn't heard the plane. She didn't hear the rest of what was said, either, but she'd heard enough.

Now she had to pull herself together and stay pulled together, no matter what. Even though she was in love with Alex.

CHAPTER TEN

'JAYNE.' Alex wanted—and needed—to take Jayne into his arms, to feel again the closeness they had shared last night.

Wanted, but couldn't have. Not now.

The pilot was going over his plane, making sure all systems were go before he boarded them for the trip back to Alice Springs. There was no privacy. There'd been no chance to wake with Jayne and hold her, take time to navigate through what they had shared.

Alex didn't understand where last night had put him. The tangle of sensation and emotion that had gripped him had put him out of his depth, had taken him by surprise and he hadn't felt prepared to deal with that, to know himself and understand himself in that. Alex still didn't understand. The urge to try to buy time with Jayne was strong. He wasn't ready for the 'morning after' but it was here anyway.

Alex had woken as the plane had come in to land. It had killed him to let go of Jayne then, but she'd been sound asleep and he couldn't leave the pilot to walk in on them.

'I slept through his landing.' Jayne didn't quite meet Alex's gaze. Her shoulders were tight, her expression set and sombre as she joined him in the shade of an awning over the hangar. Everything was covered in dust but at the moment the air was very still so at least they could see and breathe.

'Do you regret—?'

'About last night—'

She broke off and her gaze did meet his then, and there was so much defensiveness and need to protect herself that Alex stood, stunned, because Jayne shouldn't need to feel like that. Not with…him. And because he had felt like that at times in his life before Brent and Linc had got him out of the orphanage.

What filled Jayne with that kind of fear? What about them, or last night, made Jayne feel this way? Because Alex didn't think this was about the past for her. But maybe it was, because what did he know about how Jayne felt about that?

'Last night was…special.' The words seemed to be wrenched from her.

'It was for me as well, Jayne.' He hadn't had time to come to terms with his feelings about it. Alex knew he didn't want that to be the end for them. He knew that much as he looked into her eyes.

'We had…an agreement, and maybe last night wasn't the smartest idea.' Jayne seemed to force herself to go on. 'I won't apologise for it or try to prove myself, but that was a "once" thing.'

Alex frowned. Prove herself how? Apologise for

what? And what did *he* want? He wanted to continue this intimacy with Jayne, but it was pretty obvious that she was doing all she could to push him back to arm's length.

The hurt that moved through him sliced deep. Something told him the burn would be a whole lot worse when he'd had time for it to fully register. It shouldn't hurt like that. They had had an agreement; she was right about that. And…Jayne wasn't being harsh. She looked upset by her statement, if anything. Alex didn't know what to think. Alex couldn't think.

'Ready, folks?' the pilot called from beside the plane. 'I'd like to get moving, make sure I'm on schedule for the landing.'

'I understand, Jayne.' Alex understood she was drawing a line. In the end, didn't it come down to—*Alex MacKay wasn't what Jayne Cutter wanted*?

Pride drove him to put their agreement into words that were at least halfway palatable. 'A working relationship. Don't worry. I understand the disparities. We wouldn't work out as more in the long-term.'

'No. We wouldn't.' Jayne tried to maintain a calm, confident expression as she responded. He'd said *disparities*. No doubt he meant the difference in their ages, in Jayne being older. The concept of the older woman and the 'toy boy' that had seemed half thrilling just days ago now cut her to the quick. Well, what had she been thinking to imagine he would want someone who had a decade on him in age, at his young age of twenty-five?

That kind of female fantasy was clearly for movies and those silly TV shows that had no relation to reality.

In the broad, unforgiving light of day, Alex was quite clear in what he didn't want. Jayne had started the conversation, that was true, but he'd been quick to agree with her. 'All I want is to get back to Sydney now so I can put my proposal to my father. I phoned him just now, before I came out to speak with you. He knows I'll be bringing you in for the meeting on Monday.'

She thought she did quite well to get the words out in a calm, even tone.

They boarded the plane and started the first leg of the journey out of here and back to Sydney.

CHAPTER ELEVEN

'WELL, this is an unexpected turn of events, Jayne. I would have thought you'd realise how wrong it was of you to offer your services to a rival company behind my back,' Jayne's father said as she stepped through the doors into the company boardroom. It was Monday morning. Her father stood at the end of the room beside the bay window. Eric stood beside him.

Alex entered the room behind Jayne—close enough to hear her father's words. It wasn't the way Jayne had hoped this meeting would begin, and Eric wasn't helping, standing there looking smug and self-righteous.

'Dad, Eric, I'd like you to meet Alex MacKay.' Formalities first. Then explanations. And then her proposal. Jayne didn't even want Eric here for this but, in his usual way, her father had allowed it. 'Alex owns and runs an export business here in Sydney that sells a large variety of gift-styled items to a number of wholesale and retail purchasers globally. As I mentioned on the phone, Dad, Alex is here today to add his knowledge base to the presentation I'll be bringing to you.'

Her father sat down at the head of the boardroom

table. Eric sat to his right! Jayne wanted to shake her head, but she kept her thoughts to herself.

Alex's fingers brushed over the back of her hand briefly as they, too, took seats.

It was just a touch.

But it wasn't just a touch, was it? It was Alex knowing exactly how tense she was and sitting at her side, ready to jump right into the middle of all this with her, even though her father had just dropped a highly insulting bombshell on Jayne. She was embarrassed and upset, but she had to get on with this.

And Alex reacting this way didn't mean that he loved her. He was a good man—a kind one. That was what it meant.

On the way here, Jayne had asked Alex about his talk with his brothers.

'I told them everything. They're going to go out to meet Morgan with me. We'll probably all take a couple of days once your meeting's over.'

Get it done straight away. He'd left it at that, and they'd talked more about the meeting with Jayne's father. She'd done everything she could to prepare for it, but Jayne hadn't expected her father to attack her the moment she got in the door. What had Dad heard? And from whom? Jayne knew the Lis wouldn't have spoken with him; she'd asked them to give her time to discuss the situation with her father.

'Dad, I talked to you about a number of ideas to move the company forward, and—' Jayne glanced at Alex and quickly away again '—make us really cutting edge.'

It was hard to look at Alex, hard to know she had all of his support for this, but there was an invisible line drawn between them now. He didn't want an older woman, didn't want those parts of her that were not in his age bracket. Jayne had done what she could to support him while he researched his history but he'd resolved that now, too. He'd got his answers, he was content to get to know Morgan, find out a little more about his past, bring his brothers into that equation, so for him it would all balance out once again and he could move forward. Not all miraculously fixed, but with a resolution, just the same.

Alex had been through enough emotionally just lately. He didn't need Jayne dumping more of an emotional load on him and what was there to say, anyway? She was the one who'd started ruling that line between them. Alex had merely helped her finish it. She'd drawn it because she'd known she couldn't hold a man his age, couldn't hold Alex, hadn't ever been able to hold—

Not now, Jayne!

No. Not now. Now, she had Dad to deal with. Eric's unwelcome presence to contend with. Alex's wonderful pillow gifts to talk about and the improvement of Cutter's Tours to talk about. She had her partnership to push forward for.

And do you still want that above all else, Jayne? Is it still the be-all and end-all of what's going to make your life complete? Do you truly believe that once you get this promotion you'll feel satisfied? Will it change how your father is the next time he decides to let Eric influence him? The fact that Mum left? Your inability to trust anyone to love you enough?

She was thirty-five years old. Mature enough that she shouldn't have these kinds of issues.

Jayne didn't have them. She had a business propoal— a job to do—and it had to be done now.

So keep it together, Jayne. And when this is done you can thank Alex and get things sorted out so that his supplies to the company can work and then you can get on with the task of truly pulling yourself together. One piece at a time if you have to!

Jayne held her father's gaze. 'I spent the week away gathering the final pieces of information I needed to present my proposal to you. It's true that while I was away I accepted an offer for some contract work, but it is completely doable. All I'll need is three days a fortnight. I can work later on other days, if necessary.'

'You were away revealing our company secrets to a rival company,' Eric said in a snide tone. 'I heard about this from a reliable source. There was a university student on that bus who is a friend of mine. He heard you talking shop with those business people.'

Great. The same student who'd wanted to know all about Jayne's relationship with Alex? Jayne wouldn't be surprised. 'If this friend knew who I was, why didn't he say so?' Jayne turned to her father. 'Why didn't you mention that you knew I'd been on the tours this week? Well, it doesn't matter. I've told you why I was there. Yes, I discussed the tourist industry with a couple on the tour, but I can assure you I did not reveal any inappropriate information about Cutter's. I would never do that.'

Perhaps her father read the determination and the hint of offence in Jayne's expression. He knew she was loyal to the company! At any rate, some of his anger seemed to fade. 'Perhaps you should explain.'

'I was made an offer to do some work that will mean minimal changes to my employment here, and will be a coup for me that should make Cutter's proud, Dad. It's voicing virtual tours that will be marketed to Japanese businessmen when they come over here for working vacations. These will be marketed direct to companies. It's not a slice of the pie that Cutter's would ever get. There's no crossover. Just…a coup for me and…by association…for Cutter's.'

'I see.' Dad still looked surprised and not particularly happy. 'Perhaps you should explain everything you've been doing.'

He had barely stopped speaking when Eric broke in. 'This is still something that should have been discussed first.'

'Maybe you should be quiet and allow Jayne to do that with her father now.' Alex's words were flat, yet Jayne still sensed protectiveness and support in them.

And her heart melted because, even though she had tried not to let her emotions free when she'd met Alex outside the building this morning, Jayne was still utterly conscious of him and of the feelings she held inside her heart for him, whether they were painful or not.

She had to remember that these protective and

supportive emotions from Alex did not equal love. Care, yes. But not love. Jayne's heart wrenched as the thought found its mark. She wanted to fall to pieces. She admitted that, but she couldn't do it. Especially not now.

So Jayne looked her father in the eyes, ignoring Eric, and told him about the work she'd be doing for the Lis and then she put her proposal to her father.

Dad listened.

Eric listened.

Alex listened. Whether her father and Eric appreciated or even approved of his presence at this meeting or not, Jayne didn't care because she felt his support, even though that was crumbs from the table compared to what her heart longed for from Alex.

But Alex gave what he had for her in relation to her work—unstinting support for her in that. And that was something Dad…didn't give to Jayne. Hadn't given.

Today Jayne was asking her father for that support.

She handed the floor to Alex to elaborate on his company's contribution to her plan.

When he was done, she turned to her father. 'What do you think?'

'It's a good plan. Extensive but doable and I can't see how it wouldn't do the company's bottom line good, overall.' He seemed a little shocked.

Maybe he hadn't realised all that Jayne was capable of, that she could pull this proposal together quickly and on her own. 'I worked on all of this by myself, Dad, from home in my own time. The last two big jobs I've done, you've given credit to Eric for some of the work on those when he hadn't contributed much at all. I did this by myself so you would clearly see that it was all my work, not Eric's.'

'Why would you worry about that?' Her father shook his head. 'Eric is a good worker. You shouldn't be jealous of his position in the company, Jayne. You and Eric can share the workload.'

'In this case, we didn't,' Jayne said flatly. 'With my last major project, you made the commitment to promote me to partner when that project was successfully completed. Instead, you held back on the promotion, saying you wanted to focus on Eric's career. I'm your daughter, I've worked here a lot longer, I have more experience and I'm not willing to be put off from that promotion again. This proposal comes with my request that you formally appoint me to the partnership position. I've worked for it. I've more than earned it. I think this proposal speaks for itself that, as an employee, I'm worth it.'

'That's asking a lot.' Eric spoke the words half beneath his breath, but Jayne heard them.

At his side, Alex stiffened.

Jayne held her father's gaze. 'Dad?'

Her father's gaze shifted between her and Eric. 'Maybe at the end of this year—'

'No.' His words were empty; he was trying to placate her. Even after all Jayne's efforts, even after bringing this fabulous proposal to the table, he'd looked at Eric, this newcomer 'golden child' whom he…what? Wanted to treat like a son? Treat better than his daughter?

Hope disintegrated.

Jayne glanced at Alex. She wasn't embarrassed to have him here, to know that he'd heard this. That surprised Jayne but…they'd been lovers, had shared intimacy, had shared Alex's most emotional moments, too. And Jayne loved him. If anything, it was too easy to let Alex in to the deepest parts of her. 'Don't worry, Alex. You'll still have your part of this proposal.'

'That's not what's on my mind.' Alex cleared his throat and turned to her father. 'Sir, with due respect, show me anyone but Jayne who's brought this kind of plan to you?'

'It's all right, Alex.' To be championed by him…

Jayne wanted to throw herself into his arms and just forget all of this. Well, those arms weren't hers. They'd been on loan for a night. That was all. And if she couldn't get her father over the line with her request for a partnership—

'I don't need this kind of stress and pressure right now, Jayne.' Dad's words came with a shake of his head. 'Katie only left months ago.'

'And I'm sorry about that, Dad.' Jayne was sorry, but Dad's most recent wife leaving wasn't her fault. Dawn leaving hadn't been her fault. Jossie and Evelyn leaving…not her fault. Mum leaving…

Not your fault, Jayne. Never your fault.

Jayne drew a breath and her voice was firm when she spoke. 'I'm sorry, Dad, but I'm not to blame for any of your relationship breakdowns, and I've worked hard for the company and have earned this partnership. I'm not prepared to keep asking for it. I've presented you with a brilliant proposal that will take the company forward. In return for that, I want my promotion to partner.'

'You're grooming me for that position, Rod.' Eric's tone was chummy. 'Really, it's not right for a woman. Not in Cutter's.'

It was the most bigoted statement, but Jayne refused to be sucked down into any kind of justification by this man. 'You're a long way behind me in skills and in experience, Eric.'

She turned to her father. 'By all means review the proposal. I think, in light of the importance of this, it might be best if I take a few more days off while you deliberate.'

Her chin lifted. 'I'm rather feeling the need to re-group, Dad. You've delivered a blow today, whether you realise it or not. I'd like your response by the end of Wednesday. After that, we can see where we are with everything.'

'And if that answer isn't what you want to hear?' Dad glared at her, though Jayne thought that might have partly been because she'd forced him into a corner he hadn't expected.

'If not, then I'll be looking for work elsewhere that will fulfil my career goals and supplement the work I'll be doing for the Lis.'

Jayne got to her feet, indicating the meeting was at an end. Dad and Eric rose too and, in a corner of her mind, Jayne noted the irony of their compliance.

'We can always still take Mr MacKay's business,

whether your ultimatum is acknowledged or not.' Eric spoke the words as a parting shot.

Jayne opened her mouth to respond, to say that was exactly what she wanted, but Alex got to his feet, joined her near the door and his hand moved to the small of her back as he answered. 'Jayne's proposal is offered with the condition that my company will take this work on only if she receives her long overdue partnership. Sorry if we didn't make that quite clear.'

'Alex…' The one low word passed through her lips, appreciation and warning all at once.

But he simply opened the boardroom door and stood back. 'We're leaving now, Jayne. We're finished here. The proposal is delivered. Your brilliant plans are unveiled. Your father can take a better look and see for himself just how much money these improvements will bring to the company. And then, even though you'd already earned it before now, he can reward your years of service and hard work with that partnership. I look forward to you hearing from him to that effect before the end of Wednesday.'

Jayne wanted to stop and tell him she wasn't prepared to let him lose this work because of the demands she'd made on her father. That hadn't been part of her plan.

'It's all right, Jayne. We'll talk about it once we're out of here.'

The walk from the building to the underground car park passed in a blur. Once they were in Alex's four-wheel drive Jayne drew a deep breath and acknowledged, now that the meeting was over, her legs felt a

little shaky and she felt just the slightest bit light-headed.
'Even though I'd told myself if my father denied me the
partnership this time, I'd leave and forge a new career
elsewhere, in the end I truly didn't expect that. I've
worked my heart out for the family company. Eric's...
just an outsider.'

'He seems to have your father's ear.'

'Dad mentioned Katie. That was his most recent
wife.' Jayne stopped herself in time from calling Katie
a child bride. 'When Katie left and Eric started working at Cutter's it was as though Dad transferred all his
energy from his broken marriage to taking Eric under
his wing.'

'When your father should have been taking more
notice of what he had in you in the first place.' A thread
of anger came through in Alex's words.

Anger for Jayne, even though this meeting had left his
own plans in possible danger. His understanding brought
Jayne to the brink of the emotion she'd been trying to
hold back since she'd first walked into that meeting.
And that emotion expanded to include all of her love
for Alex, and then Jayne truly did feel overwhelmed.

When they stopped outside her building all she could
think was to try to keep it together until she got inside.
Now...wasn't a time to lean on Alex too much, to expect
things of him, to want him to look after her needs, meet
her needs. No person had done that in her life. Why
would that change now with a man who, whether she...
loved him or not, didn't feel the same way about her?

Don't humiliate yourself by reaching for too much with him, Jayne.

She'd done her share of that in life—had reached to her mother, her father, only to be rebuffed by Mum and rebuffed in the workplace by Dad, even while he allowed her to climb ranks in the company.

Only *some* ranks. Dad held back on the partnership in the same way he held back on allowing Jayne completely close in their father/daughter relationship.

Jayne tightened her emotions and hoped she could keep them together. Alex was a wonderfully supportive person to know in business. It was up to Jayne to only look to him in relation to work, and right now she couldn't think too much about that, either. She reached for the door handle and turned to look at Alex. 'Thank you for attending the meeting with me. When I hear from my father, when I get the final verdict from him—'

'Whatever it is, we'll deal with it.' His glance held so many emotions at once before he blinked and there was his usual steady gaze with all his other expressions tucked away in the backs of his eyes.

Jayne must have imagined the depth of some of those expressions straight out of her love for him and how much she wished that love could be returned.

She…hurt too much. She needed to pull herself together. 'I'll be in contact about the work for Cutter's. I hope you enjoy your trip to the outback with your brothers.'

'What will you do during that time, Jayne? I can put

the trip off until after you hear from your father.' He hesitated. 'Or will you see one of those friends that you spend time with?'

'That's all finished.' The words came out before she could stop them, straight out of her knowledge that she couldn't go on in those empty involvements any more. How could she after being in Alex's arms?

But Alex had to make that trip and he had to get back into his work as well. 'It's important that you make the journey.' She tried for a light tone. 'You'll have another chance to get the adrenalin rush that someone your age can enjoy so much, too. Another driving trip where you can pit yourself against Mother Nature.'

She was trying to point out the differences, to remind him of those. 'I'll…I guess I'll look into job possibilities.' She was fairly certain she was going to need them. 'I can cope financially, Alex. I wouldn't want you to worry about that. Even on the income from the work with the Lis I'd be fine. I have savings plus an inheritance tucked away from my late grandmother who passed away before I was born.'

Jayne had received every provision, really. She'd never lacked for food or shelter or worried where the next meal might come from. But she'd felt lack and loss in her life, just as Alex had. She couldn't take any more loss—or dragging out of hope, and more hope only to have it dashed in the end.

Some people might say it was just work so what was the big deal? But it wasn't only about work. It was about her relationship with her father, a right to respect, and core needs inside Jayne to give and receive love and affection—to feel that her love was worthwhile and valued. 'I just need to focus on where I'm going from here. I can't handle anything else at the moment. I need to be by myself.'

She needed to stand on her own feet. Wasn't that the only way?

'I understand, Jayne. It's all right.' For a second she thought he looked devastated, but that didn't make any sense. He blinked a moment later and Jayne wasn't sure what she'd seen at all.

'What makes you happy. That's…all that counts,' Alex murmured.

He left then.

Jayne told herself she would not fall apart now. Because, if she started on that path, she wasn't sure if she could ever get off it, or just how low it would take her. And, with her father's attitude towards her final request to be made a partner, Jayne needed to be in a positive place, somehow, to find enough other work if she needed it.

Jayne went inside.

'You're not on your game today,' Brent said as he and Alex walked off the paintball field.

It was Wednesday afternoon. Alex should have been at work—they all should have—but they'd made their overnight trip outback for his brothers to meet Morgan. Alex had met other relatives out there and started to learn about that side of his heritage. It had gone well, but it had also been emotionally draining and, the whole time, a part of him had wanted to be back here in Sydney with…Jayne.

When they'd got back to the city, Linc had suggested they take the rest of the day off. It was a bit late to do much on the work front anyway and they all needed time to absorb the impact of the trip. Alex seemed to have an overload of restlessness and he'd quickly agreed when Linc had suggested a trip to the paintball field.

Alex now had more paint splatters on himself than Brent and Linc combined. Linc had walked a little ahead and fallen into conversation with a guy about gardening. 'I thought the activity would help get rid of the restless feeling.'

'I thought meeting a blood relative might have done that.' Brent laid his hand on his shoulder. 'In fact, I was fairly convinced it had when you told us about it the other day but you're still unsettled, aren't you?'

'Yeah.' *Unsettled* was a good word for it. This was his eldest brother, and Alex needed to spit this out to *someone* so it would stop going around in his mind and driving him insane. 'Jayne, the woman I did that bus tour with. The deal for me to provide pillow gifts for her family's bus tour company is probably going to fall through. I don't really care about that for myself.'

Money was money. Alex didn't take it lightly. It had helped bring security for him and Brent and Linc, but it wasn't everything and he had plenty already—a blooming company, good growth and economic strength.

'I'm…I don't think I'm going to be able to walk away and…leave Jayne behind.'

A bit late to feel like that, wasn't it? She'd told him she didn't want him.

His brother's face stilled. Tension mounted in the back of Brent's neck and his head twitched to the side once, hard.

Alex froze in place. As if that would somehow help Brent to control the movements that sometimes got the better of him with his autism.

As if they mattered, anyway.

Brent sucked in a breath. 'What's not working out about this?'

'She doesn't want me.' Jayne didn't want to commit. Her family life had been fractured. Maybe she wasn't able to let herself trust in a meaningful relationship.

And you can, Alex? Since when did that change?

Yet for Jayne he would take that leap of faith.

'If you feel that way about her, maybe you need to try to figure out how to keep her in your life.'

'I need to see her. She's waiting on the response from her father today, as well, as to whether he'll give her this partnership or not.' Alex's thoughts were already speeding ahead.

Didn't he owe it to himself, and to Jayne, not to just give up? There had to be some way to keep Jayne more in his life, to buy time to see her and maybe her feelings for him could grow.

'Was she happy seeing you?' Brent asked quietly.

'Yeah.' Alex thought about the way Jayne's face had

glowed when they were together, and about how happy she'd made him, too. 'She was happy with me.'

Alex and Brent stepped into the shower area. Linc was already in a shower cubicle further down, as evidenced by him singing off-key at the top of his lungs.

'Tell the king of singing that I couldn't hang around.' Alex headed for his shower. 'If I'm doing this, I'll clean up as fast as I can and then go. Considering Linc's only just getting wound up with that singing, I'm guessing I'll be gone before he's finished making his hair smell pretty.'

Brent burst out laughing, as Alex had intended.

And Alex got under the shower so he could finish here and go to see Jayne.

There had to be some way…

CHAPTER TWELVE

'ALEX, hi. I wasn't expecting you,' Jayne said as she opened her apartment door.

'I'm sorry I didn't buzz first. I walked into the building when some guy walked out.' Alex searched Jayne's face. He wasn't sure if she was pleased to see him or not. She looked tense, troubled. 'I figured it would be quicker. Have you heard from your father?'

Jayne shook her head. 'Not yet. I wanted to go out, actually, and kill some time that way, but the other side of me insists I stay here by the phone, even though I know my mobile is working perfectly well and he could call me on that.'

At least she was talking. That had to be a good sign, didn't it?

Jayne stepped back. 'Would…would you like to come in?'

Yes. And I never want to leave you.

'Yeah. Thanks.' He stepped over the threshold and into her living room.

Jayne wrung her hands together before she hastily

dropped them to her sides. She was nervous. Worried about her job future.

Well, she didn't have to go through the rest of the wait by herself. Alex could at least give her that. Company. Support. She'd said she didn't want any of her men friends. Alex wanted to draw hope from that, too.

'Can you divert your home phone to your mobile?' Alex drew a deep breath. 'There's a park less than a block away. We could go there, get you out of here for a while.'

'All…all right.' Jayne went into her office and diverted the phone, made sure she had her mobile in the pocket of her tan linen trousers and the key to her apartment in her hand, and gestured towards the door.

Jayne and Alex walked along a pedestrian track in the park. There were other people about, but Jayne didn't take much notice. She only noticed Alex.

'Why did you come, Alex?' She asked the question straight from her heart.

Was she weak, for taking this?

But this is business, Jayne. His contract could be in jeopardy.

Yet, in her heart, Jayne didn't believe Alex had come to her for only that reason. He'd told Eric and her father that he wouldn't work with them if Dad denied her the partnership. That wasn't only about work, either. But Jayne needed to address it. 'Alex, you made a sacrifice for me. If Dad refuses to give me the partnership—'

'I know I could still deal with him, Jayne, but when we first met and I told you I could do with the new work of supplying the gifts for your company's tours, I didn't mean because of money or business. I needed a new challenge and something to distract my mind from personal frustrations.' He seemed to hesitate. 'My company is always expanding and profits are rising. The work for Cutter's would have been a boon, but not desperately necessary to me. Not…at the price of your happiness.'

When she would have argued, he held up a hand. 'That's something that can be sorted out once you hear from your father.'

'Yes, I guess you're right.' A soft breeze kissed through her hair, ruffling the tendrils. 'Hopefully, that'll be soon. I've looked into a couple of jobs, but only research. I need to hear from Dad first before I know what my next step will be.'

'You could work with me, Jayne.' The words came in a low stream. 'Be in partnership with me. I know you'd be valuable.'

'That's…' Was he being kind? 'How could you benefit by giving me a partnership in your company?'

They'd walked far into the park and now they stopped in the dappled shade of a tree. 'It's a growing company. Until now, I've wanted to have complete control of it myself. I consult my brothers here and there about certain things but…' He trailed off and then said honestly, 'I know you're someone who'd be an asset. You're skilled and have years of valuable experience. I've already worked with you. I trust your integrity. If we became business partners, my company would reap the benefits of your innovative outlook, determination, commitment and drive.'

'It's a very generous offer.' Jayne appreciated that, but could she work with him, loving him the way she did, and not go crazy? Could she say no to working with him when it would mean she'd get to at least see him? But would seeing him that way, and not being able to express love to him, destroy her?

He leaned his hand against the trunk of the tree. 'And it's an offer that you can't make a decision about just now,' he said very gently. 'I do understand that, Jayne. First up, you need to hear from your father.'

'That's right.' Jayne found a grassy patch of ground. 'You don't mind if we sit? I didn't get a lot of sleep last night.'

'I didn't, either.' He sat beside her and plucked at a blade of grass with his fingers.

Even with her inner awkwardness in his presence right now, Jayne couldn't get enough of looking at him, was so conscious of his nearness. Her emotions catapulted around inside her, as they'd done the night they'd made love.

Confidence and uncertainty wrestled inside Jayne. Her job was on the line. That was stressful. Her need for Alex, to express her feelings to him, was also highly emotive. Jayne couldn't express those feelings because Alex didn't return them.

The ring of her mobile phone made her jump.

'Answer it, Jayne. It's what you've been waiting for.' Alex's calm words helped her to pull herself together, though his expression seemed as tense as Jayne felt inside.

'Hello?' Jayne got the one word out, looked into Alex's eyes.

'It's Dad.' The words came over in a stern tone.

'Hello, Dad. What's your decision?' Jayne chose not to waffle. She could hardly breathe from anxiety and uncertainty, but that was just all the more reason to at least deal with this cause for her unease. At least there would be an outcome here and she'd know the answer to this question. She glanced at Alex.

'Your ideas all have merit,' her father said cautiously.

Too cautiously?

Jayne's fingers tightened around the phone. She braced herself, even as she spoke. 'It's an excellent proposal. I'm certain you can see that.'

'I'm willing to take the ideas on board, but I'm not prepared to look at a partnership for you just yet. It's really more of a man's area, anyway, and you do already have a good position in the company, Jayne.'

'A man's position for someone like Eric?' The words burst from Jayne before she could stop them. Couldn't her father see that he was being manipulated by the man? See Jayne's value? 'You promised me that partnership, Dad. I'd already earned it. I've given my world to Cutter's—to you. I put faith in you, in being part of the family company and working towards that goal. You can't go back on your word.'

Dad blustered on. He had lots of reasons and excuses. But, in the end, he wouldn't budge.

Jayne could see disaster ahead for Cutter's because she truly didn't believe that promoting Eric through the ranks would be good for the company, yet it was clear that was what Dad intended to do, and he certainly wasn't going to listen to any advice from Jayne about it.

So this was it. Jayne drew a shaky breath. 'I'm sorry, Dad, but if that's your final stance on the subject I have to give you my resignation. I won't be back into work again.'

At her side Alex stiffened. His hand half rose from his side as though he wanted to touch her but he stopped himself before he got there.

Breathe, Jayne. Just breathe.

'That's foolish, Jayne.' Dad's voice was gruff, surprised. Totally uncomprehending, even now, despite everything. 'What will you do? You're cutting off your nose to spite your face. And the pillow gifts idea was a good one.'

An idea that Dad would lose because of this parting of the ways.

'I already have two alternative job offers, Dad. What I'll do is start somewhere new and fresh where *I'll* feel new and fresh.' And, hopefully, truly appreciated.

That thought hurt a little and Jayne quickly said her goodbyes before Dad could get angry, or she might break down. She ended the call and turned to Alex.

It took all she had, but Jayne managed to push back

her emotion and speak calmly. 'I guess there's no need to explain, and I appreciate your offer of work.'

'But you won't accept it?' Alex got to his feet and helped her up, too.

'I don't want to reject your offer but my instincts… I'm not sure if I can…it's hard…'

'Take some time.' He started them back towards the park's exit. And his thoughts seemed to turn inwards. 'Maybe I need some time, too, to think and…consider my strategy. Don't do anything rash, Jayne. Please? Give it a few days for things to settle a bit. It's been a hectic time for you.'

For him, too.

'The pillow gifts—'

'Were part of the whole deal.' His implacable expression warned her not to bother trying to negotiate the issue.

Jayne didn't know what he meant about his strategy, but he walked her back to her apartment building and she said goodbye in a bit of a daze. She'd just ended decades of work at Cutter's. Where would this put her relationship with her father? Had she done the right thing?

For all reasons?

Jayne was determined not to be scared and, really, she only had the wibbles on the inside a little.

Fibber.

But Alex let her go, and Jayne went, and she just wouldn't think about when or if she might see him again.

He'd lost a lucrative sales opportunity right along with her ending her working life at Cutter's. Could Jayne do anything about that? There must be a way...

CHAPTER THIRTEEN

ALEX had waited a week, left Jayne to her own devices for a week. In that time, Jayne had written to let him know that the Lis had negotiated to put her in charge of their tourist operations here in Australia. When she'd let them know she was leaving Cutter's they'd snapped her up.

So Jayne's future was secure. She'd be managing a tourist incentive. Alex was happy for her, but he wasn't happy. Not down inside himself where he…missed Jayne. She'd wanted to talk to him about her work for the Lis. Alex didn't know why, but maybe that desire of Jayne's would give him an advantage with his… strategy.

Alex picked up the phone and dialled Jayne's number. He had no idea whether what he had planned would work but he had to take a leap of faith and try.

Answer the phone, Jayne.

'Hello? Jayne speaking.'

Just the sound of her voice was enough to squeeze his heart. Alex drew a breath. 'Hi. It's Alex. I need you to do something with me, Jayne.'

'What is it? What can I do to help you?'

'I need you to come outback with me again. Just one piece of unfinished business out there that could be to both our advantages.' He paused. 'You said you wanted to speak to me about the Lis. That can be done out there as well, if you like.'

'I'll help you with whatever business you need to conduct. Is it delicate? Do you need a woman's presence? Or a translator for a tourist or visitor?' Did Jayne sound somehow disappointed?

'It's a proposition, yes.' Not for business, but he would use whatever advantages he had to get her there. 'I really do need you for this, Jayne. No one else will do.'

'I'll help you. You helped me, Alex. You dropped everything to go on tour with me.'

'I had my reasons, too.' But he just went on, 'And now I'm asking you to fly to Alice Springs and meet me there. If I make bookings for you, can you be there tomorrow morning? The second flight out of Sydney? Can you spare the time before you take up your new job?'

'I'll…be there.'

'Oh, Alex. This is a place Morgan showed you?' Jayne asked the question in a hushed tone the next day. 'While you were out here with your brothers?'

Jayne had thought Alex wanted to take her back to Uluru or maybe to an artists' settlement or something. She'd been prepared to help him any way she could. He'd earned her support and, as Jayne had come to grips with leaving Cutter's, with her father's limited support and his choice to groom a man for partner over all Jayne's hard efforts, it was important to her to do the right thing by Alex, whether seeing him made her heart ache or not.

She didn't want to think of this as saying goodbye. If Alex agreed to her suggestion, it wouldn't have to be that.

And now, instead of meeting anyone, he'd brought her to this beautiful deep, natural pool in this isolated spot in the outback.

Alex took her hand and led her to the edge of the water and they sat side by side in the quiet stillness in the shade of a tree.

'Is your missing piece in place now, Alex?' she asked in a whisper. 'Are you reconciled to all that you've learned about yourself?'

'I was restless. I felt incomplete. That feeling is easing now.' But his serious expression remained. 'I felt guilty for feeling lost at all when I already had Linc and Brent. It's something that I pushed down and didn't want to know about, having a pocket of emptiness even when I had them.'

Oh, Jayne understood about people pushing down their deepest feelings, for wasn't it what she'd done about her father holding back from her at work for far too long?

And about other things, Jayne.

Well, now she'd stopped working there. Jayne swallowed hard. It was for the best in the end. And she didn't want to think about the rest. 'I don't think your brothers would mind—'

'They don't.' Alex gave that wry smile that Jayne had…fallen in love with before she'd even known she'd done it. And then he sobered and looked almost… nervous. 'I'm missing something else now. Someone else.'

'It's not me.' Jayne's words came straight out of all her uncertainties. Alex couldn't be missing her. Not to any degree.

'But it *is* you, Jayne.'

'Do you mean you still really want to work with me?' He might truly want that. 'Because I talked to the Lis and they really want to take on the pillow gifts plan we had and use it for their tours. We'll have to change some of the items to suit their tours, but…Dad can't use the plan we put to him.

'He forfeited that right, and I know you didn't want to work with him in those circumstances, but I didn't want you to lose the work for your company.'

'So you found a way to fix it for me.' He shook his head. 'You're incredible. Do you know that? I'll accept the deal with the gifts. And I would have loved to work with you within my own company, Jayne, but you've got a great opportunity with the Lis.'

Jayne nodded. 'I have. I was upset about leaving Cutter's and I've had a couple of unpleasant phone discussions with my father since, but my mind is made up. I've told Dad that's about work, and I don't want to lose our personal relationship.' She drew a breath.

'It may not be perfect, and Dad's going to have to put some work in to regain any of my trust now, but I don't want to lose what I do have with him. And I'm starting to feel excited about moving on to the Lis.'

Jayne had come to a crossroads in her working life. She'd made her choice and another path had unfolded for her. She'd also made a choice about meaningless involvements and she admitted that quietly. 'I want to spend more time with my sister, too. I love her and my niece, Cora. I want the relationships that I have to be meaningful so…I've also let my men friends know that I won't be socialising with them any more. Because they weren't meaningful.'

'I'm happy to hear that, Jayne.' He searched her face. 'I think you'll only find joy in spending more time with your sister and niece, too.'

'Thank you.' She drew a breath.

'There's a special reason why I brought you here, to the middle of the outback, to this place, Jayne.' Alex's expression had sobered and he spoke the words in a deep tone edged with determination and…

Jayne wasn't sure what else. 'What is it?'

Alex's lashes lowered before he met her gaze again. 'This place has special meaning to Morgan's…to my heritage. When Morgan brought me here, he said the pool would help me know what I needed in my life.'

'To know who you are. You have worked that out. Your heritage.'

'Those things, yes, but they're not everything.' He gave a slight shrug. 'I don't know if I believe in this place in quite the way Morgan does, but I respect his beliefs and his age and wisdom, and I *have* sorted out my thoughts and it did seem fitting to bring you here.'

Jayne's heart began to beat hard. 'I'm not sure if I understand.'

Alex took her hand and squeezed. 'I found *you*, Jayne. You wanted a company to provide pillow gifts for Cutter's Tours. That company was mine. We came together through that link.'

Though the words were about business, the look in his eyes was not. The meaning behind the words was not. Could he mean—?

'I fell in love with you.' His admission held a deep tone of conviction. 'I never expected that to happen in my lifetime—with any woman. I didn't think I knew how to love a woman. Not like that.'

Jayne hadn't expected that to happen to her, either, but it had and now that she'd heard Alex's words—oh, she wanted to believe in them but could he really be certain of his feelings?

One side of Jayne wanted to reach for Alex, to hold him, hold *this*, but how could she do that? 'You're twenty-five. How can you truly know what you want? How can you know this isn't just a phase for you?'

He shook his head and met her gaze. 'You know better than that. We may have known each other a short time, but it's been an honest, open time where both of us have revealed things about ourselves that others wouldn't have seen. Where we've faced deep issues and had to deal with them whether we wanted to or not. In different ways, I'm as mature as you are. You pointed out our age gap but what's that matter in the end? It's ten years. Some couples have double that gap between them. Why does it matter so much to you? If it's because of your father, you're not responsible for his relationship choices or their outcomes.'

Jayne didn't answer straight away. Could Alex be right? Had she used her father's messy relationships with younger women as an excuse for avoiding committing to a man?

She'd fallen for Alex and it was partly the fact that he was younger that had made Jayne afraid to fully trust in how he might perceive her. 'You're in the prime of your twenties and that shows. You're a highly attractive man and I suppose I was conscious of no longer being that young, of beginning to age and perhaps not being quite perfect in some ways.'

His eyes widened with shock that bordered on in-comprehension. And then they narrowed. He said very firmly, 'I don't want to hear you say anything like that again, Jayne. When I first met you, I thought how beau-tiful you were. Inside and out. I loved your elegance. That was something a younger woman wouldn't be able to have no matter how she tried, because your maturity and life experience are part of it. You should only ever celebrate your age and be proud of all it means. That you've lived. I value that, Jayne. It's very attractive to me.'

He meant the words—Jayne could see that, see his sincerity. She'd felt so threatened by the difference in their ages, by body image and wrinkles. And, deeper still, by the fact that two very key people in her life had not truly been able to freely love her.

Deep down, Jayne knew she had to admit this to Alex. To be brave and do that.

'I felt insecure when Mum left, and because Dad couldn't let me close the way I wished he could.' She finally admitted it. 'I blocked myself off from the idea of commitment with a man because I didn't believe I'd find somebody who would love me for myself.'

'I've felt threatened by being younger than you. Matching your age isn't something I can do. If you wanted that...' He drew a breath. 'I tried to get you to work with me so I'd be sure I could keep seeing you, but I need more than that with you. I need all of you, Jayne, if you can find those feelings inside yourself for me.'

And in that moment, out here in the clarity of the out-back with nothing but this still pond and red dust plains and silence and sky over them, Jayne finally stopped worrying about the little things, and even the bigger things, and put her trust right out there. 'I'm in love with you, too, Alex.' She finally allowed the words to come out. 'I realised it the night we were trapped out here and we...made love. That wasn't like any other experience I'd had. I knew it was something special and when I woke in the morning and...missed you, even though you were just outside, I knew what was inside my heart. I let my fears get in the way. I thought you didn't feel the same way, that in the light of day you'd looked at me, at my…age and it wasn't attractive to you.'

She hadn't expected to find someone she wanted to spend her life with. But it had happened anyway.

He shook his head. 'I didn't understand my feelings at that time, but that had nothing to do with attraction. You're stunning to me. You always will be. I thought you were rejecting *me* because of my age, or because I couldn't be what you wanted.'

'No.' She bit her lip as a memory stirred and warmth made its way to her cheeks. 'Actually, when we first met I found the thought of being attracted to you, an older woman to a…younger man…exciting. I felt bad about that because of my father, but…it was there.'

A slow smile spread across his face and a hint of devilment came and went in his eyes. 'I can work with you feeling like that about me.' He sobered. 'It's not something that will ever worry me, Jayne. I'll only ever be proud to be at your side.'

Jayne laughed and tried to push back her blush and then she, too, sobered. 'If I do this, Alex, if I give you all my love, it will be for ever. I won't be able to control that.'

But she'd already given it. Her heart had given it. Her mind just hadn't been ready to catch up and acknowledge what had happened. A smile started to tug at the corners of Jayne's mouth until it finally, tremulously broke through. 'It's too late to worry about controlling things or making up excuses, isn't it? I'm already there.'

'I'm there, too, and I'll make it worth it for you, Jayne.' His hand rose to touch the sides of her face, to cup her chin and there was so much love, so much emotion in that touch, in the way he held her. So much gentleness and so much strength and so much commitment...

He drew a deep breath. 'I can't love you any way other than with what's inside me, and that's...everything.'

'I love and need you, too, Alex. And...I think we can be stronger together than we would be apart, and that we can go forward together and be happy together. I want to live with you, handle all these family-related ups and downs with you as they come along. Things aren't great with my father at the moment. He's angry that I resigned and...I'm angry that he didn't value me more but I'm still hopeful of a decent relationship outside of the office, given some time for both of us to cool down a bit. Maybe if I'm not working with him there'll be a better chance for that.' Jayne was willing to try. For now, she knew what she needed. 'Most of all, I just long to be with you.'

'I want to marry you, Jayne. I want all of it.' He drew a breath. 'I...need to hope and believe that, despite anything around us or whatever we're up against, we can build a life together and be strong.'

'It's what I want, too.' Jayne knew it. Oh, way deep inside she knew it with every certainty, every part of her. 'So I will marry you, Alex. We'll plan it and we'll do it, and we'll work together on everything else, too.'

She drew a tremulous breath. 'Would you consider a baby one day?'

Alex stilled completely and an awe-struck expression crossed his face. 'A son or daughter with you. Yes, Jayne. I would want that.'

Alex drew her to her feet and she looked into his eyes with the backdrop of the Australian outback all around them, a vast vista filled with secrets and possibilities, harshness and durability and changes and things that never changed. Filled with Alex's history, and hers too, because this country Australia was home to both their hearts.

And Jayne knew she would come back here with him again and again to remind both of them of all they could do and be together. Jayne had a suspicion that Alex's uncle Morgan had known exactly what he was doing in bringing Alex here.

Because she and Alex had found the beginning of the rest of their lives together here.

And Jayne couldn't be happier.

As Alex took her into his arms and lowered his mouth to hers, Jayne gave herself to those emotions and knew he was doing the same.

This *was* their beginning.

* * * * *

Coming Next Month

Available November 8, 2011

#4273 SNOWBOUND WITH HER HERO
Rebecca Winters

#4274 THE PLAYBOY'S GIFT
Teresa Carpenter

#4275 FIREFIGHTER UNDER THE MISTLETOE
Melissa McClone

#4276 BLIND DATE RIVALS
Nina Harrington

#4277 THE PRINCESS NEXT DOOR
Jackie Braun

#4278 RODEO DADDY
Rugged Ranchers
Soraya Lane

HRCNM1011

REQUEST YOUR FREE BOOKS!
2 FREE NOVELS PLUS 2 FREE GIFTS!

Harlequin®

Romance

From the Heart, For the Heart

HRI1B

Harlequin® Special Edition® is thrilled to present a new installment in USA TODAY *bestselling author RaeAnne Thayne's reader-favorite miniseries,* THE COWBOYS OF COLD CREEK.

Join the excitement as we meet the Bowmans—four siblings who lost their parents but keep family ties alive in Pine Gulch. First up is Trace. Only two things get under this rugged lawman's skin: beautiful women and secrets. And in Rebecca Parsons, he finds both!

Read on for a sneak peek of CHRISTMAS IN COLD CREEK. *Available November 2011 from Harlequin® Special Edition®.*

On impulse, he unfolded himself from the bar stool. "Need a hand?"

"Thank you! I…" She lifted her gaze from the floor to his jeans and then raised her eyes. When she identified him her hazel eyes turned from grateful to unfriendly and cold, as if he'd somehow thrown the broken glasses at her head.

He also thought he saw a glimmer of panic in those interesting depths, which instantly stirred his curiosity like cream swirling through coffee.

"I've got it, Officer. Thank you." Her voice was several degrees colder than the whirl of sleet outside the windows.

Despite her protests, he knelt down beside her and began to pick up shards of broken glass. "No problem. Those trays can be slippery."

This close, he picked up the scent of her, something fresh and flowery that made him think of a mountain meadow on a July afternoon. She had a soft, lush mouth and for one brief, insane moment, he wanted to push aside that stray lock of hair slipping from her ponytail and taste her. Apparently he needed to spend a lot less time working and a great deal *more* time recreating with the opposite sex if he could have sudden random fantasies about a woman he wasn't even inclined to like, pretty or not.

"I'm Trace Bowman. You must be new in town."

She didn't answer immediately and he could almost see the wheels turning in her head. Why the hesitancy? And why that little hint of unease he could see clouding the edge of her gaze? His presence was obviously making her uncomfortable and Trace couldn't help wondering why.

"Yes. We've been here a few weeks."

"Well, I'm just up the road about four lots, in the white house with the cedar shake roof, if you or your daughter need anything." He smiled at her as he picked up the last shard of glass and set it on her tray.

Definitely a story there, he thought as she hurried away. He just might need to dig a little into her background to find out why someone with fine clothes and nice jewelry, and who so obviously didn't have experience as a waitress, would be here slinging hash at The Gulch. Was she running away from someone? A bad marriage?

So…Rebecca Parsons. Not Becky. An intriguing woman. It had been a long time since one of those had crossed his path here in Pine Gulch.

Trace won't rest until he finds out Rebecca's secret, but will he still have that same attraction to her once he does? Find out in CHRISTMAS IN COLD CREEK. Available November 2011 from Harlequin® Special Edition®.

brings you
USA TODAY Bestselling Author

Penny Jordan

Part of the new miniseries

RUSSIAN RIVALS

*Demidov vs. Androvonov—let the most
merciless of men win...*

Kiryl Androvonov
The Russian oligarch has one rival: billionaire
Vasilii Demidov. Luckily, Vasilii has an Achilles' heel—his
younger, overprotected, beautiful half sister, Alena...

Vasilii Demidov
After losing his sister to his bitter rival, Vasilii is far too
cynical to ever trust a woman, not even his secretary Laura.
Never did she expect to be at the ruthless Russian's mercy....

The rivalry begins in...

THE MOST COVETED PRIZE—November
THE POWER OF VASILII—December

**Available wherever
Harlequin Presents® books are sold.**

Harlequin
Super Romance

Discover a fresh, heartfelt new romance
from acclaimed author

Sarah Mayberry

Businessman Flynn Randall's life is
complicated. So he doesn't need the
distraction of fun, spontaneous Mel Porter.
But he can't stop thinking about her. Maybe
he can handle one more complication....

All They Need

LONGER
BOOK
Same Price!

Available November 8, 2011,
wherever books are sold!

www.Harlequin.com

HSR71742

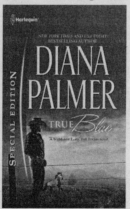